DEFY

KINGS OF RETRIBUTION MC MONTANA

SANDY ALVAREZ

CRYSTAL DANIELS

TWO PENS-
CRYSTAL Daniels
Sandy ALVAREZ
-ONE STORY

<h1 style="text-align:center">1</h1>

<h1 style="text-align:center">LOGAN</h1>

"Motherfucker." I throw the socket wrench in my hand across the shop. It ends up hitting a shelf full of miscellaneous used motorcycle parts. For the life of me, I can't concentrate on a damn thing. This rebuild shouldn't be taking me as long as it has. Usually, I would have been done with something like this more than a week ago. No, these days my mind is elsewhere. It's on my woman.

Life with Bella has been more than I could have ever imagined it being. I've walked through hell and back for her. Overcome incredible odds in order to hold her every single night. I'm prepared to dance with the devil himself if that's what it takes to give her everything.

Are there days her sassy mouth overloads her little ass? Yes.

Does she want to defy me on everything? Every. Fuckin'. Day.

But I wouldn't have her any other way. Bella makes me feel more alive than I've ever felt in my life, but this past year hasn't been easy for her—for either of us.

More than anything I want to have a family and grow old with her. Unfortunately, life seems to think otherwise. For months we've been trying to start a family of our own. So far...nothing. I'm all in. I want it as much as she does, but the stress of it all is starting to take its toll.

"What's crawled up your ass this morning, brother?" Quinn quips from the other side of the shop while under the hood of a pickup truck.

Still irritated I fire back at him, "Fuck off, Quinn."

"What the hell is going on out here?" Jake's voice echoes off the shop walls.

Undeterred, I start to walk over to find the socket wrench I threw so I can get back to work.

"Sunshine here is having another bad day, Prez," Quinn remarks as he wipes the grease from his hands.

"Logan. Office. Now!" Jake barks.

Turning on my heels, I follow Prez through the shop and into his office.

"Close the fuckin' door," he orders.

I know by the tone of his voice, he is fed up with my attitude. I've been lashing out for a while now. I'm aware of it, and so is everyone else. I think I'm about to get a verbal beatdown. I don't want to hear it, but I've had it comin'. Tense as fuck, I continue to stand with my arms crossed over my chest.

"Sit the fuck down. I ain't lookin' up at you while we have a chat," he gruffs.

Reaching down, I grab the back of the chair and drag the legs across the linoleum floor and plant my ass in the seat.

"I've been overlooking this shit attitude of yours for several weeks now. Always coming in ass draggin' on the floor and snappin' at everyone. Plus, you're behind on work." Jake pauses, giving me time to answer him.

Letting my head fall back I stare up at the ceiling. "You're right, I've been a big dick lately."

"Talk to me, son."

Leveling my head, I scrub my hand down my unshaven face. "Bella and I are having a rough time trying to start a family. Doctors can't find a reason she can't get pregnant. It's taking its toll," I tell him the short version.

He leans back in his chair. He looks tired. I'm not the only one going through something. I can't put my finger on it because Jake is so tight-lipped about his personal life, but something has had him stressed these days as well.

"It will happen when the time is right, Logan. You're both young."

It's nagging at me. I haven't shared the piece of information I'm about to reveal to anyone. Mostly because the timing hasn't been right. I wasn't about to overshadow all the positive things happening around us. But I need someone to talk to about it. I swallow past the lump in my throat. "Several months ago, Bella suffered a miscarriage." I hang my head in sadness. It feels good to talk to someone and to acknowledge our loss finally. I look back up at him. Sadness mars his face. "She had found out she was pregnant by taking one of those home tests, but before she could go to the doctor to confirm it, we lost the baby," I tell him.

I remember both days like they happened yesterday. Bella and I find time every weekend to take a ride on my bike; always ending up at the lake. Bella wore a smile that outshined the sun all day, which in turn made my day even better. While sitting on the ground with her between my legs, we sat in silence. As the hues of golds and reds danced across the surface of the water, Bella spun around, wrapped her legs around my hips and reached into her back pocket.

"Close your eyes," she said as she leaned forward and whispered in my ear.

A smile tugged at my lips, and I played along. Lifting my hand, Bella slipped what she had been holding onto my palm, and I wrapped my fingers around the object.

"Open your eyes," she said softly.

My gaze fell between us to look down at my unopened hand. When I opened it, the word 'pregnant' stared back at me from a white and blue stick.

I felt it.

My heart skipped a beat.

When I lifted my head, I took her in. The woman I love. "I'm gonna be a dad?" I would have never thought I could feel so many emotions at once. I wasn't prepared to be so overwhelmed. She bobbed her head up and down giving me a definite yes, then I kissed her.

Nothing could have prepared me for what happened a few days later. She wanted to wait until she confirmed the pregnancy with a doctor first before sharing the news with everyone. The following week, two days before her appointment, she woke up in the middle of the night with terrible cramping and spotting. Worry set in, so we decided to go to the emergency room. A few hours later we were back home. She was utterly devastated, and so was I.

Bella was having a miscarriage. I held her until she cried herself to sleep. The one sound that crushes me more than anything in this world is the sound of her crying.

"Why didn't you say anything, son?" Jake lets out a hefty sigh.

"Because her sister had announced at her wedding, she and Gabriel were going to have another baby. Bella's miscarriage was a week before that, and she didn't want to take anything away from Alba and Gabriel's happy news. So, she asked that we keep it to ourselves for a while. A while turned into weeks and then into months. The timing was never right," I explain to him.

Jake gets quiet. The silence in the room is welcoming.

"I could preach that you should have leaned on your family during your loss, but I won't because I didn't either."

I look at him confused.

"Your aunt miscarried twice. Both early in the pregnancy. I wanted to be a father so badly." His eyes start to get a distant look in them. "She would have made a great mom. I suppose it wasn't meant to be. She clung to you though. You were the child she could never have, and she poured all her love into you. Eventually, I did the same. You became the son I always wanted."

What Jake just shared leaves me speechless. I mean, I know they never had kids, but I never thought they couldn't have them. My aunt was my second mom, and I've always looked at Jake as the father figure in my life.

"Like you, it got to me at times. The hurt would turn into anger. Never at her, because I kept the pain to myself. She shared it with your mom, but I don't think she ever told anyone else. I understand more than you know what you're going through and feeling, Logan. I've been there," he bares a piece of himself to me. "You need to take some time off from work—from life for a while."

"We are swamped around here. There is no way I can take time off from work now," I explain. Maybe I should say fuck it and leave town with Bella. I could contact my dad and see about using the house he has in Aspen. A place away from everyone and everything to get back to us. To finally take the time we need to heal. "I'll stay late to finish the bike I'm working on now. I'm not sure how long I'll be gone, but if you're certain you guys can hold things down around here, I might be gone by the end of the week," I tell him.

"You come back when the time is right," Jake affirms. Standing, he pulls me in for a hug and claps me on the back.

I leave his office feeling somewhat lighter than I did before. The rest of the day goes smoother than it has in weeks. I finally find my groove, and by nightfall, I have the bike finished, and I'm closing the shop.

On the ride home, I reminisce about the last trip I took Bella on. It was right after her sister went to college. Never being anywhere outside Montana, I took her to the Bahamas. I booked a small cottage right on the beach, secluded enough it felt like we were on a deserted island. Seeing her in a bikini every day was a bonus. We only stayed for one week, but it proved to be the best week of my life.

Eloping never crossed my mind. I always assumed Bella wanted to have a big wedding, yet one night as we were sitting on the beach watching the sunset the mood struck me. I turned to her, and the words fell out of my mouth, "Marry me tomorrow." I hadn't even sucked in a new breath of air when she turned her face toward me with a smile and said, "Okay." I was dead serious. It turned out; she was too. Oh, I knew she was going to get some lip from her sister and her friends, and I mentioned it to her. She, in turn, said, "It's about what we want." And, she was right.

The next morning, we went to town and picked our wedding bands out together, and I found someone who could marry us at sunset. The only thing I wasn't allowed to see was the dress she stopped to purchase.

That evening I stood alone with the officiator at sunset just outside our cottage and watched her walk toward me. Fuck, the image of her still steals my breath. I couldn't tell you what type of material the dress was or who designed it; I only know that it looked like it fit her body like it was made just for her. It was an off-white, goddess-like dress. All I could process at that moment while standing on the white sand beach was each barefoot step she took toward me was one step closer to touching her. One step closer to our forever. An entire week I had her to myself with no distraction.

Returning to the present, I lay the hammer down eager to get home.

2

BELLA

I look down at the precious baby girl cradled in my arms and into blue eyes that mirror my sister's, and I feel an ache in my chest. A pain. A longing. Valentina Martinez was born a little over three weeks ago. She is beautiful with her pale skin, jet black hair and the bluest of eyes. I'll never forget the shock of finding out Alba was pregnant the first time, but once she had Gabe and I saw the way she was with him; it was clear my sister was meant to be a mother.

It's incredible how far we have come in just a few short years. If someone had told me three years ago that we both would be married to bikers and my sister would have two kids, I would have said they were out of their ever-lovin' mind. Now though, I couldn't imagine my life any other way.

Sitting in the rocking chair in the nursery, I brush my finger gently over the top of Val's soft hair, and I watch as her eyes grow heavy. And it is not lost on me that it could have been my baby I was holding. Mine and Logan's baby would have been the same age as Valentina. Fate had other plans for us, though. We lost our baby at twelve weeks. Logan and I decided to wait until after my first appointment to announce my pregnancy. We were chomping at the bit to tell our family, and we only had one more week to wait. Our announcement never happened. I miscarried four days shy of my second trimester.

One week later, Alba and Gabriel were married, and she announced they were expecting baby number two. The news had been a blow to both Logan and me. We were over the moon happy for my sister and Gabriel but couldn't help the feeling of hurt. To this day, neither one of us has told our family about our loss. I told Logan I didn't want our devastation to overshadow my sister's time of celebration. Logan and I were each other's rock during this time. Some days having to put on a brave face is harder than others, but so far, we have been weathering the storm.

Reaching up, I wipe away a tear making its way down my cheek.

"Bella, what's wrong?" a concerned Alba asks, walking into the room.

I wave my hand at her trying to brush off her question, "I'm fine. Just happy is all." It's not a total lie. I am happy, but I can tell by the look on my sister's face she is not buying it. Her next words prove I'm right. "Liar," she blatantly calls me out.

Sighing, I stand up and ignore her statement as I walk to the crib with my niece in my arms and carefully lay her down. Satisfied she's not going to rouse, I make my way out of Valentina's room with my little sister on my heels. When we make it to the living room, Alba speaks up once again. "Please tell me what's wrong, and don't tell me nothing, Bella. You haven't been yourself lately. Don't think I haven't noticed. You're my sister. I know you. I've been waiting for you to talk to me. I'm not waiting anymore. I want to know what's going on with you."

When I give her an irritated look, she adds, "Don't look at me like that. If this were the other way around, you'd force me to talk too."

She has a point there.

Sighing, I take a seat on the couch, and Alba follows suit. "You know I'm happy for you... right?" I ask.

My sister scrunches her brows together, "Of course."

As I'm about to open my mouth, Alba grabs hold of my hand. "I know you're struggling with something, Bella."

And that's all it takes. My sister's words make me crumple into her arms and sob. I was stupid to think I could hide my feelings from her. She knows me, just as well as I know her. She understands me. Alba knows how happy I am for her and how in love with my nephew and niece I am, but on the inside, my heart is aching. Though no one knows of our loss, they all know how long we have been trying to start a family of our own.

I don't know how long I go on with my sister holding me as I cry, but soon the tears stop, and when I pull back and look at her, I see nothing but understanding. Using the sleeve of her shirt, Alba wipes the tears from my face. And when she dries my tears, I confess the secret I have been keeping from her. The one that has been eating me up inside. "I had a miscarriage."

Dropping her hands to her side and looking at me in shock, Alba asks, "What... when?"

"Just before you and Gabriel got married. Logan and I wanted to wait until the doctor confirmed everything. I was around twelve weeks," I confess.

Placing her hand over her mouth, I see my sister fighting back her tears. "I'm not even going to ask you why you never said anything. I already know. And I will tell you now, Bella. Don't ever keep something like that from me again," she says with love and anger all rolled into one.

I shake my head in protest. "You were getting married, and then after the wedding, you and Gabriel announced you were pregnant with Val. I couldn't bring myself to put a damper on your happiness. I couldn't do that to you, Alba."

Cutting me off, Alba stands up from the sofa, all but yelling, "I don't care what's going on in my life, Bella! Our whole lives, it's always been you and me against the world. When I hurt, you hurt. When you're happy, I'm happy. We may be married now, but that is one thing that will never change between us!"

She's right. We are married now and have our husbands, but nothing can ever take away the bond we share as sisters.

Standing up from the couch, I wrap my arms around Alba. "Promise me you will never keep a secret like that from me again," she whispers into my neck.

"Never again," I promise.

I'm in my car on the way to the hospital to have lunch with Emerson when my mind drifts back to the visit I just had with my sister. I feel a little bit lighter after finally coming clean with her about my miscarriage. I even told her about mine and Logan's struggle to conceive after the loss of our baby.

When we first decided to start trying for a baby, we were having fun. We would sneak off on lunch breaks, and Logan would take me to the lake and make love to me under the stars. Everything was perfect. Now our sex life has been taken over with fertility doctors, calendars, and ovulation tests. The spontaneity is gone. And even though I know Logan and my relationship is solid, our clinical sex life is a dark cloud looming over our heads. I feel it, and he feels it. The problem is, neither one of us is saying anything.

Alba suggested Logan and I talk about everything. She's right. This whole situation is going to drive a wedge between us if we continue to stay silent. We need to get back to us. That means no more doctors—no more sex schedules and worrying about when I'm ovulating. Logan and I have to make our marriage a priority. Somewhere along the way, we lost a little bit of ourselves, and I am determined to get it back.

Pulling up to the hospital, I park and fire off a quick text to

Emerson letting her know I'll meet her in the cafeteria. We have become quite close over the past couple of years. She works a lot of hours, so I make it a point to come as often as I can to have lunch with her. Eating in the hospital cafeteria is more accessible for her, so that's where I'm going now. When she is not working, she and I will catch a movie or go shopping. She has slowly been opening up to all the guys and even comes to the clubhouse on occasion. Though she still won't give Quinn the time of day. Walking into the cafeteria, I spot her from across the room when she lifts her hand giving me a wave.

"Hi," I greet her with a smile sitting across from her.

"Hey yourself. Here, I already got yours," she says sliding a plastic container with a salad across the table.

"Thanks. The next one is on me," I tell her before taking my first bite.

"How's Alba and the baby?"

I smile again. "Perfect. Val is beautiful, and Gabe is a mess. I swear that boy is his father made over. He's so serious about everything." I laugh.

After a few minutes of catching up, Emerson is quiet for a moment. I've come to know her well, and I can tell by the look on her face, something is bothering her. "Alright, talk to me Em," I encourage.

She lets out an exhausted breath. "I really shouldn't talk about this, but I had a pregnant woman in labor come into the ER yesterday. Immediately, I could tell she was on something. She delivered a baby girl early at thirty-four weeks."

Reaching across the table, I squeeze her hand. "Oh no. Is the baby okay? Did she make it?" I choke out. She is a strong woman to cope with the things she deals with on a daily basis.

"She did make it. She's upstairs in the NICU. I can deal with a lot of tragedies, Bella, but babies..." She trails off shaking her head. "When I did my NICU rotation, it was by far the most challenging time in my life." Meeting my eyes, Emerson visibly swallows. "You want to know what the worst part is? Her mother abandoned her. After she was born, she didn't even ask about her. She didn't care if she was dead or alive. Not even twenty-four hours after she gave birth, she up and left."

My hand covers my mouth in shock, and I feel anger bubble up in me. Here I am, a woman who would give anything to have such a precious gift yet struggles to conceive and then you have a woman that can blatantly leave her baby behind.

Using her napkin to dry her tears, Emerson apologizes. "I'm sorry, Bella. I didn't mean to unload all that on you. Sometimes certain cases get to me."

"Don't apologize for something like that. You know I'm here for you anytime you need to talk. Don't keep your emotions bottled up inside." *Like I've been doing.* Emerson knows nothing about my miscarriage. Aside from my confession to my sister, I haven't told anyone.

"Thank you, Bella." After a moment of silence, she speaks up again. "I've been going to check on the baby every chance I get. The NICU is low on volunteers right now, so I try to visit all the babies when I can."

"What kind of volunteers?" I ask.

"It's something we call Cuddle Buddies." Emerson goes on to explain, "Parents who have a baby in the NICU can't always be by their baby's side. Moms are discharged and have to go home and leave their children behind. It's difficult not to take your baby home. So not only is the volunteer giving comfort to the baby but the parents as well. When a mom or dad is at home or work, they have the comfort of knowing their son or daughter is getting the attention they deserve. A volunteer must hold the baby, rock them to sleep, feed them. A lot of the time the baby will cry simply because he or she needs someone to hold them, and it's hard for a nurse to give too much-undivided attention to one baby when she has several to tend to. Then you have babies like the one I was just telling you about. She's going through withdrawal from whatever her mother was on. She is having a hard time."

By the time Emerson is through explaining the program to me, my heart is breaking. And it's also telling me I need to help. I can't explain it, but there is a voice inside me telling me this is something I need to do. "I want to help," I say without hesitation.

Giving me a big smile, Emerson nods. "That's wonderful, Bella."

"What do I have to do? When can I start?" I ask.

"I can walk you upstairs now if you'd like. There is paperwork to be filled out, and of course, an interview and they will require a health exam. We can't take any chances of the babies getting sick. Their immune systems are weak. Are you okay with all this?"

We walk side by side out of the cafeteria. "Yes. I'll do whatever is necessary. I want to help."

Having Emerson vouch for me sped up the process, so a few hours later I've filled out all necessary paperwork, been interviewed and had a check-up. I was informed that everything looked good and that I could come in tomorrow for my first shift. I told the hospital evening shifts were good for me. I can come over every day after I'm done working at the garage.

Walking out of the hospital, I make my way across the parking lot toward my car. A sense of peace washes over me. It's time to take all the energy I've been wasting on stressing over mine and Logan's struggles and put it toward something positive. Sliding into my car and letting the top down, I close my eyes a moment feeling the warm breeze on my face and smile. It's time to go home to my husband.

The sun is beginning to set as I pull into mine and Logan's driveway. I don't see Logan's bike, so I know he's not home from work yet. Walking into the house, I head upstairs with determination. When I walk into the master bathroom my eyes fall to the counter where it's littered with ovulation tests, pregnancy tests, and an abundance of vitamins. Reaching down, I pick up the small trash bin and begin chucking everything into it. No more damn tests. No more damn vitamins. Just, no more.

"Angel, what are you doing?" Logan's deep voice asks from the doorway, startling me.

"I'm exhausted, Logan," I say, giving him a quick glance before continuing the task at hand. "I love you; Logan and I want us to have a baby more than anything, but I'm tired. I'm sick and tired of all this shit," I declare. "I'm tired of the planned sex. I'm tired of the disappointment after yet another negative pregnancy test. I'm sick of what our lives have become." Stopping what I'm doing, I set the trash bin down and look up at my husband. His expression is not one of anger or sadness. No, he looks relieved. That very look is all I need to see to know I'm making the right decision. "I miss us," I admit.

Covering the distance between us, Logan stands toe to toe with me and brings both hands up to cup my face. "I miss us too, Angel."

A split second later my breath hitches when I see heat flair in Logan's eyes and his mouth crashes down on mine. Fisting my hands in his hair, I bite down on Logan's bottom lip causing him to growl. The next several seconds are a dazed frenzy. We begin tearing at each other's clothes. Once I pull his shirt over his head, Logan grabs a hold of mine ripping it open. I faintly hear buttons hitting the floor at the same time I work at unbuckling his belt, before reaching inside his jeans freeing his already hard cock. The sight has me licking my lips wanting a taste.

Reading my thoughts, Logan says, "You can have my cock in your mouth later, babe. Right now, I need to be inside you."

Once he rids me of my shorts, Logan swipes his hand across the bathroom counter causing everything to crash to the floor. Picking me up by my ass, he sets me down on the edge where he pulls my panties to the side and buries his cock inside of me with one thrust causing me to scream out his name.

"So fuckin' wet," he rasps pulling all the way out leaving only the head of his cock inside me, making me whimper in protest.

"Look down, Angel. I want you to watch as I fuck you," he demands. And I'm all too eager to listen. I immediately look down at us and watch as Logan's thick cock slides in and out of me.

"That's it, watch your husband fuck your tight pussy."

Logan's dirty mouth fuels my impending orgasm and I feel myself begin to clamp down on his cock.

"Not yet. You don't come until I tell you to," Logan orders.

"Please, I need to come," I beg.

"Not yet, Bella," he growls while digging his fingers into my hips, slamming into me so hard my head thumps into the mirror behind me.

"Logan," I start chanting. Bringing his hand between us he uses his thumb to rub over my swollen clit, and I can no longer hold back.

"Fuck, Angel," he grinds through clenched teeth right before he buries his face in my neck. I throw my head back and scream out my orgasm at the same time Logan plants himself deep inside me and roars his release.

This...this is what we have been missing.

3

LOGAN

After tying up a few loose ends at the shop, I decided to ride out to my dad's place. Earlier this morning I got a text from Nikolai telling me our dad was flying in and wanted to see both of us. His timing is perfect because I plan to ask him if he has a place, I can take Bella away for a few days.

Knowing Bella and I are on the same page with the baby making has done wonders with the stress I've been under. The two of us getting out of town is a much welcome idea.

The gate opens as I make my way down his long driveway. I pull up alongside my brother's car and park my bike. As I begin to climb up the steps, the front door opens.

"Ah, it's good to see you, son. Come, let's catch up," my dad greets me.

After he pulls me in for a quick hug, we make our way into the living room where Nikolai is relaxing in a deep-seated leather chair next to the fireplace.

"Logan, good to see you. Would you like a drink?" he asks me.

"A cold beer sounds good," I reply, sitting down on the couch. Leaning back, I stretch my left arm over the back of the sofa and stare out at the water through the large window. I come out here at least once a week to hang with my brother, that is when he isn't spending time together at the club. I've watched how well he has adapted to being here in Polson over the past couple of years, and how much he loves his job with the construction company. We've also gotten to know each other, and there are definitely a lot of layers to Nikolai Volkov.

Handing me my beer, my dad takes a seat beside me. "It feels good to see you both."

My brother chuckles as he sips his glass of bourbon, "We talk at least once a week, Father. What is there to miss?"

"Yes, but that is not the same as being here, son." Leaning forward, he places his elbows on his knees and swirls the amber liquor in his tumbler, "I've decided to make a permanent move to the States," my dad adds.

Nikolai and I exchange a look of confusion. I'm the one to question him as to why. "Everything okay? The family in danger?" It's one of the first assumptions that come to mind. Maybe because trouble seems to weasel its way in lately wherever my family is involved, so I guess you can say I'm a little defensive.

"No," he tells us sternly and with conviction, then smirks, "I'd like to see someone try and touch my family. Death would be swift," he finishes.

I know who Demetri Volkov is and what his reach can and will do to those who oppose him or stand in his way. It's the rest of the world who never wants to know.

"To be honest, I want to be with my family, my boys. And I'm bored. I can run things from here for awhile. I'll fly back when needed," he tells us.

I'm not about to question him further. By the look on my brother's face, he doesn't look too thrilled with the new-found information. He has gotten used to having the place to himself, minus the staff. Setting his glass down, Nikolai stands and walks over to the window. He was silent for a moment before turning around to address our father.

"Who are you leaving to run things back home?"

I watch as my father's expression changes. "Sergei is under strict orders to always report to me. Always. Nothing has changed. You are questioning my decision?"

"It's not you I question. I've never liked Sergei. You are aware we never got along. I don't trust him." He looks at our father.

Leaning back Demetri sighs, "I have others watching as well, son. He has given no reason for me not to trust him. Sergei has been loyal to this family for many years. He is like a brother to me."

I feel so out of place right now. Clearing my throat, I cut through the tension building between the two of them. "I wanted to ask a favor," I direct my attention toward my dad.

"Name it." His baritone voice comes out smooth and relaxed as he sinks back against the couch.

"I would like to take Bella somewhere for the weekend." I rub the back of my neck with my right hand. I feel awkward asking a personal favor from him, "You have a place we could use for that purpose?"

He smiles. "I have several. You want something in the States or out?" he asks.

"Something close," I tell him.

He sits for a moment and rubs the scruff that has grown on his face. "I have a place in Seattle. Would that be suitable?"

It's drivable. "Yeah, that would be great," I inform him.

"Then it's settled. I'll make some calls and have the place ready for you. Everything okay with the two of you?" He studies me.

It felt good to open up a little to Jake. Talking to Quinn helped as well. Maybe I should share it with my dad and brother as well. "We've been going through a rough patch. Not with our relationship, but with trying to start a family. A while back Bella suffered a miscarriage before we could confirm and share the news with everyone. Keeping it from everyone has taken its toll on us," I confide in them.

My brother sits back down. His attention focused on me right along with my dad.

"I'm sorry to hear of this, son. My money is at your disposal. Doctors and specialists, whatever you should require we can get," my dad assures me.

Nikolai leans forward in his chair, "I'm your brother, Logan. You could have talked to me," he says with sincerity.

I sigh and shift my positioning on the couch, "We didn't share with anyone. Too much going on. We didn't want to overshadow all the good happening around us," I tell them.

"Why don't you go to Bella, tell her about your plans. Things will work out. This I know. I feel it. Just know we are always here for you, Logan. We have plenty of time to continue to become the family we are meant to be," Demetri finishes.

He's right. We are all still trying to navigate being family and learning to be a father, son, and brother. Nearly an hour later I leave my father and brother's place and head home. Bella should be back by now.

When I pull up in the driveway, she is climbing out of her car. Rolling up beside her, I usher for her to climb on. She doesn't ask why. With a bright smile she climbs on and wraps her arms around my waist, and I take off toward our place.

By the time we arrive, the lake is aglow from the sun dipping in the sky. As always, I help her off and grab the rolled-up blanket from the back of the bike. We walk to our usual spot, spread the cover, and sit with her between my legs. We let the quiet and stillness seep into our souls for a short time before I begin to tell her of my plans for the weekend. "I took some time off from work. Mostly the weekend."

"You could use a break," she responds and pulls my arms around her a little tighter.

"When we get home, I'm going to need you to pack your bag. I'm taking you out of town," I tell her.

"For how long?" she questions.

"Just for the weekend, Angel. My dad has a place in Seattle we can use."

Silence engulfs us once more. I know what she is thinking. What that bastard from Los Demonios did to her happened in Washington. I'm hoping she has healed emotionally enough to return to the state.

She sighs. "I'll be with you, and that's all that matters."

I kiss the top of her head. We continue to watch the sunset through the trees. Just as the horizon turns from burnt orange to a deep purple, we pack up and hit the road. We ride for another hour until the sky is so black all you see are the stars blanketing the night sky before heading home.

4

BELLA

I can't believe Logan is taking me to Seattle. When I came into work this morning, Jake called me to his office. He sat me down and confessed Logan told him about our situation. He also said he ordered Logan to take some time off and then ordered me to do the same. I happily agreed. I'm sure Logan has already talked to Jake about our upcoming trip. Logan and I need to decompress. This getaway is very much needed.

While sitting on a stool at the counter, placing an order for parts on the computer, I close my eyes and my skin prickles at the memory of Logan taking me in the bathroom. My husband owns me—mind, body, and soul. His body reminded me of what passion is supposed to feel like. It's been far too long since I have felt that.

"How ya doing darlin'?" Quinn asks from behind me, bringing me back to the present.

Looking at him over my shoulder, I give him a warm smile. "I'm doing okay. What about you?"

"I can't complain, sweetheart, though I'd be doing a hell of a lot better if a certain someone would feed me. I'm starvin'," he says rubbing his hand over his flat stomach. Rolling my eyes, I hop off the stool.

"Come on," I motion for him to follow me, "I brought leftover fried chicken and mashed potatoes from home. And if you're a good boy there might be some chocolate cake in there for you too," I tell him as he follows me into the break room.

"Hell yeah, that's what I'm talkin' about. Bring it on, woman." Chuckling, I make my way to the refrigerator pulling out the containers I brought from home.

Most nights when I cook, I find myself purposely making extra for Quinn and Jake and bring it the next day for lunch. If by any chance I don't bring them something they both sulk around the shop the whole day acting as if I kicked their puppy. I suppose it's my own fault though. I spoil them, and they have become accustomed to it.

"I don't know how you eat so much, Quinn, and never gain any weight," I joke as I scoop potatoes onto the plate before placing it in the microwave.

"I'm a growin' boy, sweetheart." He grins, sitting down at the table.

"You're a pain in the ass is what you are. But I love you anyway," I tell him, setting his plate in front of him.

With a look of nothing short of brotherly affection Quinn says, "Love ya too, darlin'."

I sit in the chair across from him, with my plate, and we eat together in comfortable silence. Once Quinn has finished every bite of food, he pushes his plate away then leans back in his chair, letting out a groan indicating his tummy is now full. After a few beats, he breaks the silence. "You excited for yours and Logan's trip to Seattle?"

"Yeah, I can't wait." I beam.

Leaning forward, he braces his elbows on the table. "You going to be good with going back to Washington?"

Of course. Quinn hasn't forgotten. It's exactly like him to ask and make sure I'd be okay. When Logan mentioned the trip, I'll admit I was a little apprehensive about going back to the state where I suffered so much. "It's time to go back there and make some happy memories. I will not let what happened keep me from doing so. I promise. I'm okay. I've always wanted to go to Seattle. I already have a list of things I plan on dragging Logan's ass to do."

Clearing his throat Quinn gives me a small smile. "Logan told me about what you all have been going through darlin'. I'm really sorry."

I drop my gaze to my lap and choke back the tears threatening their way to the surface. "Please don't be mad at him for talkin' to me. He was having a rough day yesterday, and we were in the break room having a beer after work and everything just sort of came out."

Expelling a deep sigh, I tell him, "I'm not upset that he told you. You are family, and we don't have any secrets. Losing our baby was not something we intentionally tried to keep from everyone. It's just with Alba getting married and the announcement of her and Gabriel expecting again, it didn't feel right. You know."

"Yeah, sweetheart, I get it," he says with understanding.

Jake walks into the room, "Somethin' smells good here."

Laughing, I point to the microwave, "Yours is in there."

When I turn my attention back to Quinn, he gives me a megawatt smile and a wink. I truly have the best family.

Leaving the shop at the end of the day, I climb into my car and head to the hospital. I have been calling Emerson daily to check up on the baby girl she told me about the other day. The one whose mother abandoned her. Today is the day she turns two weeks old. When I told Logan of my plans, he was completely supportive. With my paperwork and background check completed, today is my first day volunteering. I'm nervous and excited at the same time. Though I know I may be spending time with other babies, she is the one I'm looking most forward to meeting. Something about her story is calling to me.

Stepping into the elevator, I press the button for the NICU floor. I give them my name once I arrive at the nurses' station, they've been expecting me. I follow a nurse who introduced herself as Shelly.

"It's nice to meet you, Bella. Let's get you suited up and sanitized." I pull on a yellow hospital gown over my clothes and follow the strict hand washing instructions given by Shelly, then she leads me into the NICU nursery.

"Have a seat in the rocking chair," Shelly says pointing to a chair beside an incubator. I resist the urge to lean over and look in. Something inside me wants to wait until this sweet baby is in my arms before I look at her face. "Dr. Evan has mentioned you have taken an interest in our Baby Doe."

Nodding my head, I answer her, "Yes, I would like to meet her if that's okay?" I say sitting in the chair.

"Wonderful," Shelly beams, clasping her hands together. "The poor thing has had a rough start, but she has proven to be a fighter. She definitely has a will to live. Let me get her for you."

I watch as the nurse carefully, yet expertly, reaches inside the incubator and picks up the little girl known as Baby Doe. My heart aches at the thought of an innocent life lying inside this hospital without as much as a name. Without anyone to claim her, to love her. Pushing those thoughts away, I hold out my arms as Shelly steps in front of me, placing the baby in my arms.

As soon as I cradle her to my chest and her eyes open, I swear with everything I am, time stops. I can't explain it. All I know for sure is that at this moment my life is forever changed. I have this overwhelming need to take care of this baby. To protect her. I don't know how much time passes and how long I sit here rocking this precious bundle in my arms, all I know is I never want to put her down.

"Mrs. Kane," the nurse interrupts me sometime later. "I'm sorry, but visitation hours ended thirty minutes ago," she informs me.

"Oh, I'm so sorry. I didn't realize it had gotten so late."

"It's alright. You two looked so content, I didn't have the heart to tell you earlier. I figured a few extra minutes wouldn't hurt," the nurse says with a wink.

"Well, I appreciate it." I smile. Looking down at a sleeping Baby Doe, I kiss her forehead with a promise to return soon before Shelly takes her from me and places her back in the incubator.

With every step I take in the opposite direction of the NICU; I feel nothing but longing. Leaving her feels so wrong. By the time I make it to the parking lot and into my car, I can no longer hold back my tears. Every part of me is screaming to go back inside and hold her a little longer. I know that's not possible though. I knew this journey would be difficult when I signed up for it.

Emerson did all she could to explain to me, to try and make me understand how hard seeing sick babies can be, and how some babies will never make it out of the hospital. But nothing she said could have prepared me for the life changing connection I feel, and how leaving Baby Doe behind would be heart-shattering. How can a mother or any person abandon a baby? I don't know the answer to that, nor will I ever be able to understand how a person can do such a horrible thing. What I do know is I want to show that baby she is wanted, and most importantly I want to show her that she is loved.

A few more days have passed with me spending every evening at the hospital. It is now Thursday, and Emerson is sitting on the edge of my bed as I pack for mine and Logan's trip.

"So, Shelly says you have become quite fond of Baby Doe," Emerson speaks up. When I look at her, she has a look of concern.

"Yes, I have become attached to her," I say over my shoulder as I walk into my closet to retrieve my suitcase. Plopping it down on the bed, I sit down beside Emerson and let out a deep sigh. "I don't know how to explain it, Em. I feel a connection with her. Do you think I'm crazy?"

"Of course not, you're not crazy, you're human. What you are giving that baby is wonderful. With so many emotions involved, I worry about you. Eventually, the baby will get better, and she will be released from the hospital and into the care of the state."

My stomach clenches. I don't want to think about her becoming a ward of the state. The possibility she could be shuffled around from one foster home to the next. I've heard enough horror stories about the system to know of the things that can happen to that sweet baby. "Has the hospital heard from her mother or any family?"

"No, nothing. I don't think we will either," Em confesses. When I think about it, her biological mother wouldn't be a better choice than the state. "Look, let's not think about the what-ifs right now. Baby Doe still has a little longer before she will be released from the hospital. Don't worry yourself to death right now. Focus on you and Logan and this trip you are about to go on, okay?" Emerson is right, but not worrying is easier said than done. "Will it be okay if I call every day while I'm gone, to check up on the baby?"

Reaching over Emerson squeezes my hand, "Of course. I'll make it a point to stop by the NICU every day to check up on her."

"Thanks, Em," I say letting out a relieved breath. Patting my hand, "You're welcome. Now come on. You have some packing to do. I love Seattle, you and Logan will have a great time. Don't worry about anything here while you are gone. I promise everything will work out; you'll see." As I continue to pack all I can do is pray she is right.

5

LOGAN

It's been raining since we made it to Seattle. Thankfully, knowing this is how the weather can be most of the time, we drove here in Bella's car. After making our way through downtown Seattle, we pull up to my dad's building, and Bella peers up at it through her passenger window.

"Wow, and his place is at the very top? Can you imagine the view it's going to have?" She smiles as she continues to take in her surroundings. Unlike myself, Bella hasn't had much opportunity to travel. I've seen many places from the back of my bike, mostly due to all the runs the club has had over the years.

Knowing I get to give Bella many first experiences makes me a damn happy man. Using my dad's access key, I pull into the basement garage and park. Eager, Bella quickly exits the car and waits for me. With a smile tugging at my lips, I climb out and walk to the trunk of the vehicle retrieving our bags. Yes, bags. We are only going to be out of town for two nights, and this woman has packed two suitcases with my clothes just taking up half of one.

Grabbing her hand in mine, I lead us toward the elevator. Once inside, I punch the penthouse button with my fingertip.

"I talked to Leyna last night," she tells me, breaking the silence. "You mind if we meet up with her later tonight for drinks?" She turns and looks up at me.

"We can do whatever you want, Angel. It's been over a year since she left town, right?"

"Something like that. I'm excited." She bounces on her toes before pressing her body against mine as she reaches up for a kiss. Meeting her the rest of the way, I press my lips to hers. Before the kiss has a chance to go any further, the elevator dings and the door slides open revealing a massive foyer.

"Wow," Bella whispers.

It's drastically different than what we are used to. Hell, it screams money and power. I usually don't give much thought to the fact that my dad has money. I typically don't even give thought to the fact he runs a massive empire either. Sitting the bags down, we walk into the main open room. Even with the gloomy, grey skies outside, the natural light fills the room. Floor to ceiling windows damn near covers the entire space. The furnishings are very modern. Much different than his estate in Montana, which is more of a rustic, down to earth feel much like mine and Bella's home.

"Look at the view," Bella gasps in awe as she continues moving forward. "I can't believe we get to stay here for the weekend."

Standing back, I take her in.

"What do you feel like doing before meeting up with Gabriel's sister?" I walk up behind her and ask. Brushing her hair off her shoulder, I graze my lips across her neck causing her to shiver. I can think of many things to occupy our time, and each one involves us not leaving the building until it's time to go home.

"I'm a little hungry. Maybe some lunch..." tilting her head to the side, she pauses and closes her eyes while I continue to kiss her, "and shopping?" she breathes.

Chuckling, I wrap my arms around her and rest my chin on top of her head. "I love you."

"I love you too," she returns.

A few hours later—just as the sun starts to set—we make it back to the penthouse. I placed all the shopping bags in my hands onto the bed in the master bedroom. While Bella announces she is going to get ready, I take the time to explore the place a little further by walking over to the patio doors leading from the bedroom out to the balcony. The sliding doors alone are massive. Remembering the instructions my dad gave me, I find the remote for them sitting on a shelf close by. After pressing the button, the glass doors slide open without a sound. I step out into the crisp night air. Shit, this place has everything. An outdoor living room complete with a fire pit. I continue to explore when I happen upon an alcove. Tucked away in this secluded space is a high-end hot tub. A deviant smile tugs at my lip as dirty delicious thoughts run through my mind.

"Baby? Where did you go?" I hear Bella call out.

Turning on my heels, I head back to the room. "I was checking out the..." My words fall short when Bella comes into full view. I'm speechless looking at the outfit she has on. Bella doesn't show a whole lot of skin, not like this. I feel my heart rate pick up and my cock strain against the zipper of my jeans. *Holy fuck she is hot.* My woman is standing in front of me wearing a black dress that hugs her curves in all the right places. From her ribcage down to the hem of the dress, which by the way stops a hairline beneath her little round ass, are cutouts exposing her tanned skin on one side and her unfinished tattoo on the other.

"Turn around," I command her.

With a glint in her eyes she slowly spins until her back is facing me. I groan. I can't help myself. The back of the dress dips low, right to the small of her back and with her hair swept to one side shows off her wing tattoo. Fuck. I'm going to be walking around with a raging hard-on all night.

Bella looks at me over her shoulder. Catching my heated stare, she smiles.

"You like it? It's my first time in an upscale nightclub. For once dressing up means more than a sundress and a pair of boots," she declares.

"How much time do we have before we have to leave?" I ask her.

Peering at the clock, which is sitting on the nightstand next to the bed, she tells me, "About thirty-five minutes. We don't have far to go; the club is a couple of blocks from here. Why?"

I reach out my hand, and she gracefully walks to me on the three-inch heels she is wearing. "I want to show you the view outside." The sun has just disappeared, and the sky has become painted in deep purple and blue hues. I lead her to the railing and watch her face light up as she takes in the city skyline as it starts to illuminate the night with its lights.

"Logan," she gasps, "it's breathtaking."

"It is," I agree, not taking my eyes off her. Stepping behind her, I trace my finger across the tattoo at the base of her neck. Knowing how adventurous Bella can be when it comes to sex, I decide to push her limits a little more. Slowly, I tug at the tie around her neck and let my warm breath dance across her ear.

Grabbing hold of the railing with both her hands she answers me with a whisper, "Yes."

When her answer leaves her lips, I let the top of her dress fall, exposing her breasts. Her breathing picks up as I cup her breasts and run the pads of my thumbs lightly across her hardened nipples.

"Someone might see us."

I dip my head and kiss her shoulder, "It's dark enough out here they would only see shadows. Grab the rails again, Angel. We don't have much time, so it's got to be hard and fast."

She complies, placing her hands back on the rails in front of her. It's not the first time we've done anything outdoors, but the setting is much different. Reaching down, I hook her hemline with my fingertips and slide her dress up over the curves of her hips and ass only to find her pantyless. "Jesus," I groan and my dick throbs.

Sliding my hand down, I find her clit swollen and waiting for attention. Her pussy is so fucking wet. I run my finger in circles around her nub causing her to moan as her head falls back on my shoulder. I watch the rise and fall of her chest as I work her, bringing her body to the edge of an orgasm. "Spread your legs, Angel," I give her another command.

With my other hand I undo the zipper on my jeans freeing my cock and I press my swollen head against her opening, "You're mine," I growl thrusting my hips forward burying my length inside her, then slowly pulling out before surging back in.

"More," she begs, pushing her ass back against me. Growling, I give her what she wants.

Hard and fast. Just like I told her.

My grip on her hip tightens as I continue to work her clit with my other hand. Once I find my rhythm she falls in sync. I don't slow my movements. At this point, I can't. I'm completely lost in her. She feels too good. "This pussy is mine." I don't care who may be watching. Let them look.

"Oh God, Logan," she moans as her back bows, and her pussy clenches around my cock as her orgasm rips through her, causing my release to follow. I give her a few light strokes across her sensitive nub causing her limbs to quiver. "I think you like the idea someone could be watching," I comment. I tuck myself into the confines of my jeans and place the top of her dress back over her breasts and tie the strings securing it in place. Tugging the hem of her dress down over her ass and hips she turns, and I pull her body into mine, dip my head and kiss her. I feel myself grow hard for her once more. I can't ever get enough of her.

Smiling through our kiss, she giggles. "You're going to have to put that away. We're going to be late if we don't get going soon."

I groan.

"It won't take me but a few minutes to freshen up. You want to do the same?" she says as I reluctantly release her and watch her walk away.

"No. I'm wearing what I got on, including the smell of your sweet pussy."

"Good. That way every woman who tries to hit on you will know you're mine," she sasses.

Damn right I am.

Roughly twenty minutes later we are entering Rumors nightclub with Leyna in tow. It's not what I was expecting. I thought we were going to walk into a stereotypical big city nightclub. The whole color scheme is black and purple. Black leather furniture and walls painted in a deep shade of purple emphasized by the dimmed purple lights casting down on them. Without sounding too much like a woman, the place kind of exudes sex.

A barely dressed woman welcomes us, immediately addressing Leyna.

"Ms. Martinez, would you like your usual table?"

"Yes, thank you," she responds to the hostess who then seats us at a corner booth.

"This place is sexy, Leyna." Bella's comment echoes my thoughts from before.

"Sí *Yes*, I like coming here to unwind when I get the chance." She turns her face from Bella and looks at me, "Logan, how is my hermano *brother*? I haven't heard from him in a couple of weeks."

On the one hand, I can understand Gabriel's attitude toward his sister. She left town with a cop. One we don't know much about. It's not really because Taylor has a badge, it's more because we don't know much about him. Not yet anyway. You add that to the fact that she is his baby sister, you get what he is currently dishing out. He feels betrayed in a sense. I'm not going to tell her all that. I'm sure she is already aware of his reason. "He's good. Promise." I don't know what else I can say. She accepts my answers and moves on.

"So, do you like Seattle so far? Have you had a chance to see the city lights at night yet?" Leyna asks Bella.

Slightly blushing, Bella smiles at Leyna.

She saw the lights alright.

She won't be forgetting the moment for quite a while.

"The view from Demetri's penthouse is unbelievable," she tells her with a gleam in her eyes.

A waitress walks up and takes our drink orders. The service here is prompt, and we don't wait any longer than a couple of minutes before the girls are sipping on some fruity drinks and I'm swirling the amber liquid around in my glass while they talk amongst themselves. I mostly overhear the two of them talking about Leyna and Gabriel's strained relationship. Bella is enjoying herself, and I'm relaxed and content sitting here listening to the music and nursin' my whiskey. I lift my glass to my lips when someone walks up behind Leyna and puts their hands on her shoulders.

Agent. Fuckin'. Taylor.

Leyna's eyes widen, but she doesn't jump, which means she knows who is behind her. My eyes are locked in a hardened stare with Lex.

"Lex, what are you doing here?" Leyna asks.

With his eyes still locked on me, he answers her, "I'm off the clock for the night. I wanted to see **my** woman." He gets ballsy and smirks.

"I didn't tell you where I would be tonight, so how did you find me?" Leyna questions him as irritation starts to show. I want to know the answer to that question myself.

"I've got my ways," he informs her.

"Lex..."

"You're mine, Leyna. The sooner they accept that, the better. Your brother needs his ass kicked for being a dick."

I stand. "Watch your fuckin' mouth, Taylor. You threatenin' one of my brothers?" I square off with him.

"Your brother—her brother is being an asshole." He takes a step toward me.

Before things escalate, Leyna stands as well and faces him. Bella stands and stays at my side. We watch Leyna as she whispers something to Taylor and lays her hand on his chest calming him. The change in his demeanor is instant as soon as she touches him. I recognize it. Bella has the same effect on me.

Fuck.

Turning, Leyna walks over to Bella and hugs her, "It was so good to see you. Give my brother my love. I'm going to go home. Call me soon. I want to hear about the hospital and the baby."

"Of course, I will. You need anything you call. Got it?" Bella peers over Leyna's shoulder and directs her next words to Taylor, "You'd better take care of her, Lex. She is my family," she warns him.

6

BELLA

It's Monday morning, and I'm lying in bed seriously contemplating not getting up. Logan left for work about thirty minutes ago with a promise to be home by dinner time. So, since I have a full day ahead of me, I throw the blankets aside and climb out of bed. Making my way to the bathroom, I brush my teeth, wash my face, and then pile my hair on the top of my head in a messy bun.

Walking into the closet, I snag a pair of black leggings off the hanger, and pair it with a grey off the shoulder slouchy tee and my black flats. I have an appointment with Gabriel this morning over at Kings Ink. This appointment will be my last. Gabriel has done an excellent job of covering my scars. It's been a slow process, but it's also worth it. My tattoos are beautiful. Gabriel can work some serious magic. I am so thankful for the time he has spent working on me. My tattoo starts just under my left breast and angles across my abdomen, and then all the way down my hip.

The blood-red roses are a stark contrast to the black lace background. The detail in the lace is what has taken so long. A year to be exact. I'm amazed at how invisible my scars are now. It's also crazy how addictive tattoos are. I already have ideas for what I want next.

On my way out of the house, I stop by the living room and grab the gift I got for the baby off the coffee table. While Logan and I were in Seattle, I made him take me to the zoo. Yes, the zoo. To my surprise, Logan didn't argue. He said if we were together, he didn't care what we did. When we were at the gift shop picking up some souvenirs for baby Gabe, Valentina, and Mila's little girl Ava, I spotted a stuffed black bear. A bear represents strength, and I knew it would be perfect for the baby.

On the drive over to Kings Ink, I smile at the memory of the past few days. Demetri's penthouse was breathtaking. His view overlooked the entire city. My skin prickles at the memory of Logan taking me on the balcony our first night there. The next two days that followed were just as memorable. Along with the zoo, we went to the Space Needle, a waterfront Ferris wheel, and we stuffed our faces with so much delicious food that I guarantee I have gained at least five pounds. On the second day of sightseeing, I snapped a picture of Seattle's public library and sent it to Alba. If I know my sister, she's already made Gabriel promise to take her one day. Seattle is a place that has something for everyone. Logan was like a kid in a candy store when we went to one of the breweries. His exact words were *"This is what the fuck I'm talkin' about."* He also spent a small fortune on beer.

Pulling up in front of Gabriel's shop and parking, I reach over to the passenger seat of my car and grab my purse. Just as I'm stepping out of my car, I hear my phone ping with an incoming text.

Logan: *Miss you already Angel.*

Me: Miss you too.
Logan: *Have a good day. See you tonight. Love you.*
Me: Love you too.

Tossing my phone back in my purse, I walk into Kings Ink with a smile on my face. The bell alerts Gabriel to my arrival as soon as I open the door. I see him at his station already set up for me.

"Bella," he addresses me with a chin lift.

"How's it going, big guy?" I ask, making my way to his chair.

"It's going," he grunts.

Not deterred by his usual grumpiness, I continue. "How are my niece and nephew doing?" My last question earns me a smile. Gabe and Valentina are the light of their Papi's eye. You can see it whenever someone mentions his children.

"They're good," he tells me, his face going soft. "Gabe took his first steps the other night."

"What!" I balk, "And my sister didn't think to call me?" I stand there gaping at Gabriel. Momentarily stunned by my outburst, Gabriel finally speaks.

"She didn't want to bother you while you and Logan were out of town."

I plop down onto the chair beside me. "She could have called me," I grumble. After a beat, I look over at Gabriel who is getting his ink tray ready. "That boy of yours is going to give you hell now," I smirk.

"You're probably right," Gabriel chuckles.

"Come on," I tell him as I peel my shirt off over my head leaving me in a sports bra. "Let's get this last session over with."

After about twenty minutes of silence, I decide to bring up a topic I'm sure will hit a sore spot with the big guy. "Logan and I met up with Leyna while in Seattle." At my confession Gabriel stills. A second later the buzz of the machine fills the room once more, and he refuses to acknowledge what I said. "I know it's not my place to interfere, so I'm just going to say my piece, and then I'll leave it at that." When he doesn't protest, I continue. "She misses you, big guy. Leyna going back to Seattle with Lex was not something she did to hurt you." Reaching over and placing my hand on his forearm, I look Gabriel dead in his eyes. I want him to understand what I'm trying to tell him. "Leyna made that decision for her. She decided that her happiness was important. It would be nice if her big brother could have her back and be happy for her. We have no control over who we fall in love with Gabriel. You of all people should understand that." Once I've said my piece, I lie back in the chair and let him finish his work. I can only hope he and Leyna work out their differences. I know they both miss each other. Leyna had to follow her heart, and Gabriel can't help but feel betrayed. The club and the law don't usually mix.

Rubbing elbows with the Polson PD is one thing. The Kings and the local law enforcement have an understanding, but Lex... that's a whole other ball field. Lex is an FBI agent. The same FBI that has been up the club's ass a time or two in the past. Leyna told me she and Gabriel still talk a couple of times a week, and Leyna has been to visit twice, once when Gabe was born and again with Val. But he refuses to acknowledge her relationship with Lex. I hate seeing my family hurt. Besides, I've seen the way Lex looks at Leyna. He is so far in love even a blind man could see it. And because of his feelings for Gabriel's sister, I truly believe he wouldn't come after the club for anything. I don't think he would risk what he has with the woman he loves. Logan would never admit it, but I think he gained a little bit of respect for Lex when he saw with his own eyes how protective he is toward Leyna.

"Done," Gabriel announces, bringing me out of my thoughts.

Rolling his chair back a couple of feet, Gabriel snaps his gloves off and toss them in the trash bin beside his station. Standing, I walk over to the mirror and look at the finished product. "It's beautiful, Gabriel," I breathe. And it is. The red is so vibrant. A year ago, I couldn't stand looking in the mirror. And now, I can't seem to stop.

"A beautiful piece for a beautiful woman," Gabriel says as he strides over to the front counter. His comment makes me smile. He can be so sweet at times.

Pulling my shirt back on over my head and picking my purse up off the floor next to the chair I just spent two hours in; I make my way over to the counter where Gabriel is.

"Here," he says, handing me a jar of cream for my tattoo. "You know the drill." I take the offered jar and toss it into my purse, "Thanks, big guy."

He raps his knuckles on the counter. "Until next time," Gabriel nods.

"Give the babies a kiss for me, and tell my sister I'll stop by tomorrow," I say waving and giving a warm smile over my shoulder as I walk out the door.

Once I'm in my car I glance down at my watch and see I still have about an hour before I'm due at the hospital, so I decide to run to Grace's for a sweet snack. When I pull up in front of the bakery, the first thing I notice is that all the lights are off. Climbing out of my car, I make my way to the front door, and when I pull on it, it's locked. Cupping my hands over my eyes, I peer through the window. I see no signs of Grace or that the bakery was even open at some point today. The display cases that are usually full of cupcakes, cookies and donuts are empty. *Something is off.* Grace's bakery is open every day, even on Sundays.

Deciding to investigate further, I walk around to the side of the building where I know the stairs that lead to the apartment are located. Making my way up the stairs, I go to knock on the door and notice it's partially open. This is the part where I should take my ass back down and call Logan or one of the guys, but what if Grace is hurt? Making a hasty decision, I place my palm on the door and push it open. What I find is an empty apartment. The further I walk inside I take notice of a small kitchenette. Surprisingly, the apartment has no personal touches. Nothing that indicates who lives here. Not a picture...nothing. Looking to my left something catches my eye. A white dresser with all the drawers half open. When I walk over, I see the drawers are empty. Then I walk to the bathroom and flip on the light switch. Nothing. Grace is gone, and from the looks of her place, she left in a hurry. Digging my cell phone from my purse, I pull up Logan's number. It rings twice before he answers.

"What's up, Angel?"

"Logan," I say with a shaky voice.

"Angel, what's wrong?" he asks on high alert.

"I stopped by the bakery for something to eat before heading to the hospital, and it's closed. I thought maybe Grace was sick or something, so I came upstairs to her apartment, and she's gone," I finish.

"What do you mean Grace is gone?" Logan urges.

"What the fuck you talkin' about Grace is gone!" Jake booms in the background. "Fuck," Logan clips under his breath. "Babe, stay there. We're on our way."

Not ten minutes later I hear the roar of several motorcycles alerting me to the fact that the men have arrived. Jake is the first to burst through the door, and Logan is hot on his heels. I'm a little taken back. I've never seen Jake look so wild.

"Babe?" Logan says getting my attention. "Why don't you go to the hospital. The club will handle shit with Grace."

Nodding my head, I lean on my toes and kiss him. I don't question what's going to happen next. I know the guys will find out what's going on. "I'll see you at home later."

Arriving at the NICU, I go through the ritual of putting the hospital gown on and washing my hands. After a quick greeting with the nurse on duty, I sit in the rocking chair beside the incubator and wait patiently as she places the baby in my arms. I've only been out of town for a few days, and she already looks bigger...stronger. I look back up at the nurse who is standing to my left. "You took the feeding tube out."

The nurse smiles. "We took it out an hour ago. Would you like to give her the first bottle?" she asks.

"Yes!" I reply enthusiastically.

"Alright then," she chuckles. "Just let me go fix it. I'll be right back."

A minute later the nurse returns with a bottle. Taking it from her, I bring it down to the baby's mouth. I allow a few drops to coat her lips. Just enough to entice her to open. It doesn't take much coaxing before she opens greedily and begins going to town.

"Well, it looks like you two are old pros at this. I'll leave you to it."

Before I know it, an hour and a half have flown by. The baby has been fed, burped, had her diaper changed and is now asleep. Visiting hours are almost over and my time is up. Reluctantly, I stand and place her back in the incubator along with the gift I bought her. Stealing one last look at her, I sigh and wish for tomorrow to hurry up and get here.

7

LOGAN

Prez wasn't the only one whose nerves were on edge when Bella called to tell us something was going on here at Grace's. I'm going to tan that woman's ass for walking into a building alone knowing something could be wrong. Stepping outside, I pull my vape pen from my cut. You heard me right. A fuckin' vape pen. I decided I need to give up smokes and it hasn't been a smooth transition. I take a long pull from it, inhaling the vapors deep into my lungs before exhaling and watching the smoke billow.

Reid stepping out of the door catches my attention.

"Prez wants to see you."

Shoving the pen back into my pocket, I head inside. "Got anything?" I question him with Reid coming to stand at my right.

"Nothin'," Jake sighs as he runs his hand down the length of his beard. "Listen. You guys go on. I'll handle this for now. There doesn't seem to be signs of forced entry or a struggle. Only signs she left on her own," he says, doing his best to wear a mask of indifference as he deals with the situation.

The club knows he and Grace have had a thing for one another. For their reasons, they have been hiding it, fighting it. "So, you don't have any concerns? Prez, listen. We know—" I don't get to finish my sentence as Prez cuts it short with a clipped voice and a stern look of authority.

"I said I'd take care of it."

"Alright." I throw my hands up showing him I won't push the issue any further for now. "Riggs and a few of his men will be arriving in town in about three hours. You going to be at the clubhouse when they roll in?" I ask him.

Riggs is from the Louisiana Chapter. Our club is hosting them this weekend.

"I'm gonna need you to step up in my place, Logan. At least for the night," Prez informs me.

"You got it. I guess I'm heading out to the clubhouse." I turn to Reid, "Let everyone know I expect them all out there within the hour. And make sure the women have rooms ready for Riggs and his officers."

"On it," he quickly responds before lifting his chin at Prez and leaving.

Standing in place, I wait for the sound of Reid's Harley firing up and taking off down the road before letting myself be more than the VP for a moment. "If you need anything let me know, Jake," I tell him. His squared off shoulders slump slightly as he shifts his weight from one foot to the other.

"I know, son. I appreciate it, but for now I'm flying this solo. It's a good possibility she simply left."

Hurt briefly crosses his face. I want him to be happy. He deserves it. Grace brought back a fire that hasn't been in Jake for a long time. Sometimes a man needs to be left alone with his thoughts. Jake needs that now.

"I'll catch up with you later. Don't worry about hosting. We got it covered. You do whatever it is you gotta do. Remember your club —your brothers have your back," I tell him as I leave.

A few hours later I'm sitting at the bar at the clubhouse throwing back a beer with Gabriel. The brothers and the women all did a great job pitching in to get things squared away for the party tonight. When I say party, I don't mean a family get together. It will get X-rated here tonight. It's been awhile since we have thrown down and cut loose.

Over the past few months we have taken on two new girls, Ember and Raine. So far, they haven't caused any drama and Raine runs the bar like a pro. There's a story with both I'm sure. Hell, we all have a past, but it's not my job to sit them down and get to know them.

"You guys getting a sitter so Alba can hang tonight?" I ask Gabriel as he turns his bottle of beer up and downs what's left.

"Yeah, got it covered."

"You explain to her what to expect tonight. She and Bella hadn't been to a party like this before. Sometimes the men like to show what they're made of openly." It's part of club life; it doesn't happen every day or at every party, but it happens.

"Didn't have to. Overheard her and Bella discussing it," he tells me.

"I'd like to have been a fly on the wall during that conversation. Those two keep nothing from each other." Gabriel's lips turn up in a small smile but say no more about it. Yep, wish I could have been there. The women went back to my place to get ready and said they would ride in together. Bella, Alba, Mila, and Emerson; those women are thick as thieves these days. My thoughts stray to Grace. All the girls are friends with her too, but Grace never took anyone up on the offer to come out here to the clubhouse. She's always a little skittish and hyper-aware of her surroundings. When she did accept invites, it was to gatherings we held at someone's home. I hope Prez can find her and sort things out with the two of them.

"Logan, our brothers are rolling through the gates," Quinn walks in from outside and pulls his shades off his face.

"How many brothers?" I ask as I slide off my barstool ready to walk out the door. I've met Riggs and a few other brothers from the chapter before, but it's been a couple of years since I've seen them.

"Six on bikes and a cage carrying three women. I guess they brought some extra entertainment." Quinn smirks.

Last I heard he was bringing about a dozen members this weekend. "Alright, let's walk outside and welcome our brothers." As we step out the doors of the clubhouse, the rumble of their Harleys gets louder as they back their bikes up next to all the others before cutting them off. The car hauling the women is directed by Blake to pull up on the side of the building because the empty space near the tree is the closest to the building and designated parking for our old ladies when they aren't on the back of our bikes. Riggs, the Louisiana chapter's President, is ex-military, specifically a Green Beret, specializing in explosives. From the stories I've heard he's damn good. The fucker is big. Stands as tall as Gabriel and makes me feel like I need to up my game on my workouts.

"Logan, what's going on brother? Haven't seen you in almost two years." He strides over and extends his hand.

"Riggs. I'm good. How was the ride? That's a long fuckin' way to go."

Standing straighter he pulls his shoulders back and rolls his neck stretching his muscles. "Can't complain. The weather was nice. Sometimes you need those long stretches of highway. It helps cleanse my soul from time to time. Ya know?"

His accent isn't strong. Not like many Cajuns I've come across. That could be because he has been all over the world, but it's mixed up in there. The sun is starting to settle low in the sky, and they've had a long day. I decide to hold church tomorrow. Maybe that will give our Prez time to join in on the talks.

"Thought you were traveling with more men?" I ask him.

"We need some of them to stay behind. Got some dirty things happening around town. Not sure who is behind it, but I didn't want to risk leaving only a couple of men on their own."

"Gettin' that bad down there?"

"Yeah, brother. Shit's gettin' bad," he says then points his thumb toward one brother then the other who walks up beside him, "I brought Fender and Kiwi with me along with the three prospects."

I met the two of them before. Fender is standing at Riggs right. You take the rocker look and smash it together with a biker and that's who you get. He's their Sergeant at Arms. Kiwi there, standing to the left of Riggs is their Road Captain. He's about as tall as I am. I don't know much more about him except for the fact that he's from New Zealand. "Let's go inside and unwind." I lift my chin and gesture toward the clubhouse.

Riggs slaps me on the back. "Laissez Les Bon temps rouler, brother! *Let the good times roll, brother.*"

An hour later the party is starting to pick up. I lounge back on one of the leather couches located toward the back of the room waiting for my woman to arrive. She texted me almost twenty-five minutes ago to tell me they were on their way. I swirl my whiskey in my glass and lift it to my lips, savoring the warmth as it slides down my throat. The front door swings open and in walks Bella, followed by the rest of the girls.

"Jesus has come to save me," Riggs comments as the women continue to make their way through the sea of men. "You got you some fine women in Montana, Logan."

Gabriel's hand snakes out, pulling Alba to his side and Mila walks up to Reid, who proceeds to show everyone she belongs to him by laying a heated kiss on her lips. My Angel keeps walking, swaying her hips with every step. Her eyes fixed on mine. She decided to wear a dress tonight, paired with her boots. She's so god damn beautiful.

"This here is your old lady? Jesus, brother. No wonder you said goodbye to all other pussy. You lucky son of a bitch." Already halfway lit, Riggs who's sitting beside me downs the rest of bourbon in his glass and gets up just as Bella stops in front of me.

"Angel, this here is Riggs. President of our Louisiana Chapter," I introduce her to him.

He gives her a nod, "Your name, Angel?" he asks her with a grin.

Returning a smile, she tells him, "It's nice to meet you, and no, I'm his Angel. My name is Bella."

"Bella is Italian and Latin for beautiful, so both names suit you," he tells her, then looks down at me, "My glass is dry. I'm going to fix the problem. I'll leave you to it. Catch ya later." He walks off mumbling, "lucky son of a bitch."

"Come here." I pull at Bella's arm and guide her onto my lap. Raine walks over with a beer, hands it to me and then gives Bella her favorite, honey bourbon. I watch her lips as they graze the rim of the glass and then her throat works as she swallows the warm liquid. The flavor is satisfying. She moans and licks her plump bottom lip. My dick swells thinking about what I want those sweet lips locked around.

It turns out the women Riggs brought are dancers. Strippers. Off in the corner of the room, they've set up a staging area along with a pole. Their treat to us for hosting them this weekend. I'm already two glasses of whiskey in along with a few beers and Bella has almost finished her second half glass of bourbon. Knowing her, she won't drink much more tonight. Suddenly the lights dim low, and the rhythm of a song I recognize—*Closer* by Nine Inch Nails—starts to play. Surprisingly, Raine saunters up onto the stage. I watch as Riggs pulls up a chair front and center. He's been quietly watching her all night. I can't tell you much more because my focus has been on Bella and how enthralled she is with Raine's sensual movements. I start rubbing her leg, slowly working my way higher up her thigh until I slip my hand under her hem letting my fingertips caress the outer edge of her pussy through her panties. Lifting my eyes to the stage I watch Raine work the poll—seducing the men with her movements, her eyes trained on Riggs before scanning the rest of the room. Needing to taste Bella, I scoot us to the edge of the couch and motion for her to stand. While everyone is preoccupied, we slip down the darkened hallway and I push her against the wall and kiss her. Breaking away, leaving her lips swollen from mine I confess, "I need to taste you, Angel." Biting her bottom lip, her eyes search the area before landing back on mine. Her heated gaze telling me yes.

Sliding to my knees, she places her hands on my shoulders as I make work of ridding her of her panties, sliding them past her hips and down her thighs before putting them in the inside pocket of my cut. Pushing her dress up I expose her. With the darkness keeping us hidden, I run the tip of my tongue over her slit and circle her swollen clit. A whimper escapes her as I slide my fingers in and out of her with long, broad strokes. I slowly lick a path from her entrance to her throbbing clit again, and her hips buck seeking more. I capture her bundle of nerves and suck hard, and that's all it takes. Her back bows and her pussy clenches uncontrollably around my fingers. I hold her steady with my other hand as I take one last taste. Before I stand, I retrieve her panties from my pocket and help her step back into them and slide them back up covering her.

"Logan," my name breathlessly leaves her lips.

I kiss her.

She is mine.

"I love you," I tell her resting my forehead on hers.

"I love you." Her hand caresses the side of my face.

"Let's get back out there before someone comes looking for us," I tell her.

When we come back into the room, the second set with two of

the girls Riggs brought has almost finished, and I find that everyone is where they were when we stepped out. We walk to the bar and take a seat where Reid and Gabriel happen to be hanging out with Alba and Mila by their sides. Bella looks around before asking, "Hey guys, where's Emerson?"

"She was right here a moment ago watching the show with the rest of us," Mila informs her.

Fuck. The guys look at me. We all know she doesn't need to be walking around here by herself, especially with the other chapter members around. They have no idea who she is. "I'll go find her," I tell Bella.

Several minutes later after searching the inside and not finding her, Quinn accompanies me outside to look for her. She doesn't have her ride so she couldn't have gone far. We're walking around back when we hear a scuffle to our left. Cautiously, we go to inspect the noise.

"Get on your knees and wrap those lips around my cock, bitch," a slurred voice I don't recognize echoes through the darkness. It's the voice that follows that we both know.

"Let me go," Emerson whimpers just before we hear a very audible smack.

"Suck it, you fuckin' cunt!" the slurred male voice bellows.

Breaking into a sprint, we come up on Emerson pinned on her knees up against the building and who I believe to be one of Rigg's prospects with his cock in one hand and her hair in his other. Quinn walks up behind the guy and presses the black barrel of his gun to the back of the prospect's head.

"Take your hands off her motherfucker before your brains end up all over the building."

Releasing his hold on her hair, Emerson falls to her hands and crawls away. As soon as I help her to her feet, she begins to sway.

"Logan?" She looks up at me confused

"I got you," I tell her. I don't think I've ever seen Emerson drunk. Come to think of it she doesn't drink much at all. "How much have you had to drink?" I question her.

"I think I had a beer?" she questions herself. "Logan, something not right. I think something was in my drink." She tries her best to shake it off, but I still have to help her stand.

"Come on. The bitch isn't here with anyone. We were going to have a good time," the prospect says, tucking his dick back into his pants.

Lifting his foot, Quinn plants his boot on the guy's ass shoving him face first into the brick wall. "I believe her words were 'let me go'. Which means she said no you piece of shit," Quinn growls.

Shit. I can't leave Quinn with this guy. I pull my phone from my pocket and call Gabriel. He picks up instantly.

"Yeah."

"Find Riggs. Tell him we have a situation with one of his men. And send Bella out with him," I instruct.

"Got it," he replies.

Less than two minutes later Riggs is walking around the corner with my woman tucked behind him until he notices the site is secure, which earns major points with me. I hand Emerson over to Bella and let her know what's going on and tell her to take her upstairs and have her looked at. She listens and quietly leads Emerson through the back door bypassing the party through the kitchen.

Facing Riggs, I give him the run down. "Your boy here was about to rape a friend of ours. By the way she was acting, I'm willing to bet he put something in her drink as well." Quinn walks the prospect over to us and holsters his weapon on the way.

"You're fuckin' out, probate. This is the third fuck up. I'm willing to bet you're fuckin' wasted on those damn pills again too." Riggs reaches out and roughly grabs the young man's chin in his hand and looks him in the eyes. "Kiwi is going to drain your gas tank. Once he does, you're going to get on your bike and duck walk your ass off this property. You got me?"

The prospect hangs his head, knowing he's past the point of fucked up and doesn't say a word. Riggs makes a call and Kiwi finds his way out back, and the two of them have a brief discussion before he takes care of the order he was given. Riggs crosses his arms and sighs. "Brother, I'm sorry for the trouble. I should have given that boy the boot a month ago, but I tried to give him a chance—show him something better. Is there anything else I can do to fix this?" he asks me as we walk back around to the front where Kiwi is letting the gas from the guy's tank drain out into a can.

"You took care of your own man. Nothin' more needs to be done, brother," I assure him. Quinn sits the prospect down on the graveled ground next to the front door and instructs him to stay put.

"Logan, you need me I'll be upstairs," he says before swinging the door open, letting the music filter outside.

Riggs and I stand and wait until Kiwi finishes. We watch the young man walk his bike down the gravel road and out past the gates before retreating to the party. I'm done for the night, so I slowly start to shut things down, then seek out my woman to take her to bed.

8

BELLA

"Babe, don't forget Dad is coming over for dinner tonight," Logan reminds me as we both stand in our bedroom while getting ready for work.

"I haven't forgotten. Will Nikolai be joining us as well?" I ask, sitting down on the edge of the bed and slide my boots on.

"I talked to him last night, and he said he's going to be working late tonight. He and Reid are on a deadline. The guy who hired them to work on the resort has decided he wants to be open two months earlier than planned."

I look up at Logan with my mouth hanging open. "Two months? I hope this guy makes it worth their time. They are sure to be working a lot of late nights and weekends."

Chuckling Logan responds. "Trust me, babe. Reid and Nikolai are coming out on top with that deal. Declan is more than fair with his compensation. I've met him. He's a straight shooter. The club wouldn't do business with him if he weren't."

After pulling on my boots, I stand and make my way over to the closet where Logan is shrugging on his cut. "I'm proud of Reid and Nikolai. They have made their business a success."

Wrapping his arms around me and resting his chin on the top of my head, Logan adds, "Me too, babe."

"You ridin' with me this mornin', Angel or are you taking your car to work?" Logan asks me once we have made our way downstairs and into the kitchen for coffee.

This is something Logan, and I have decided to do every morning before going to work. We plan to spend an hour together before we start our day. If that means we have to wake up earlier than usual so we can implement some us time, then that's what we're going to do. Life can get so busy. It's important to set time aside just for us.

"I'm taking my car. I want to run to the hospital on my lunch break to visit the baby. I won't have time after work since your dad is coming over. I'm going to ask Jake for an extra thirty minutes to the hour I already take on my break."

Setting his cup down, Logan studies me from across the table before speaking in a soft tone. "This baby is starting to mean somethin' to you, Angel?"

I swallow past the lump in my throat. With my eyes trained on the coffee mug in front of me, I reply. "I can't explain it, Logan. My heart is drawn to her. I know it sounds crazy and you probably think it's because of everything we have gone through, but it's not. There's something about her. When I'm near her, and when she's in my arms I feel..."

"Whole," Logan finishes for me.

I snap my head up and let my eyes lock on his. The look on his face is a tender one of understanding. "Yes," I choke out.

After a beat of silence, Logan speaks again. "Tell me what you're thinkin', Angel?" he asks even though I'm confident he knows what my answer will be.

This is something I have been thinking about for days but haven't had the nerve to bring it up. "I want her," I confess with absolute certainty. "Everything in me tells me she belongs to me... with us," I add.

"Why haven't you told me how you feel?"

Sighing, I give him the truth. "I wasn't sure what your thoughts on adoption would be, and I was afraid you'd think I was crazy for feeling the way I do about her."

"You should never just assume, Angel. I want you to come to me with everything you are thinking and what you are feelin'. I would never think your feelings are crazy. And as for adoption, I'll admit that I've never given it much thought, but knowing how you feel about this baby girl you've been visiting; I think we should go for it."

Sitting across from Logan I feel my heart pounding in my chest. His last statement has rendered me speechless, and I can't stop the tears from flowing. Standing up from his seat, Logan makes his way around the table before scooting my chair to face him, then goes down to his knees in front of me and cups my face in his large hands. "Bella, I want a family with you. Whether it is by us or adoption, I welcome any children we have. If that baby girl means somethin' to you, then she means somethin' to me. If your heart says she's yours and she belongs to us, then we're going to try making that happen. I'm all in, beautiful."

At Logan's last words I throw myself into his arms. I'm crying so hard my body is shaking. After a few minutes my tears subside, and Logan pulls me back and kisses me on the lips. "I love you, Angel."

"I love you too," I breathe out between kisses.

"Why don't you take the day off work. Go to the hospital and talk with Emerson and see if she can help you figure out what steps you need to take when it comes to the baby."

"Breanna," I tell him.

"Who?" he asks with a confused look.

"I've secretly given her the name Breanna," I tell him sheepishly while looking down at my feet. "It means strong. Because she is strong and she's a fighter. I hated referring to her as Baby Doe."

Placing his finger underneath my chin, Logan forces me to look at him. "Breanna is a beautiful name." Standing up, Logan pulls me into him, and I wrap my arms around his middle. "Come on, babe. You call Emerson, and I'll let Jake know you won't be in today. Okay?"

With a nod, I kiss him one last time before he heads out the door. Once I hear his bike roar down the driveway, I walk over to the kitchen sink and splash cold water on my face. After taking a couple of deep breaths I walk over to the kitchen table and pick up my phone so that I can shoot off a text to Emerson.

Me: Hey. Are you at home or work?

Emerson: Home. What's up?

Me: Can I come over. I need to talk.

Emerson: Of course. Is everything okay?

Me: Yes. I'm on my way.

I'm not sure where to start with the adoption process, but hopefully, Emerson will be able to lead me in the right direction. I would think working at the hospital she would at least know what happens to children in situations where the parents abandoned them. She did tell me they are turned over to the state and placed into foster care. Maybe that is my first step. Becoming a foster parent.

Twenty minutes later I'm knocking on Emerson's apartment door. When she opens the door, the first thing I notice is how tired she looks. "You okay?" I ask when she motions for me to come in and I toss my purse on her sofa.

"Yeah, I'm fine. I just got off shift."

"Em! Why didn't you tell me when I texted you?" *Shit, now I feel bad.*

She waves me off. "Don't sweat it. It always takes me an hour or two to wind down enough to go to sleep. I'm not one of those people who can fall asleep as soon as their head hits the pillow," she assures. "I was just about to have some coffee; you want some?"

"No thanks, but I'll take some juice if you have any."

Walking over to the refrigerator, Emerson pulls out a bottle of orange juice and pour me a glass. Setting my glass down on the coffee table in front of me, Emerson sits next to me with her mug and tucks her legs underneath her. "So, what's going on?" she asks.

"How are you doing after what happened at the clubhouse over the weekend?" I ask her. "I hope you didn't get turned off by what that piece of shit did. I want you to know none of the guys wouldn't ever let anything happen to you. Especially Quinn," I say with concern. I hate that some asshole was able to drug her and take her outside of the clubhouse. I hate even more that I wasn't paying close enough attention to her. My stomach turns at the thought of what happened to her could have been much worse. Thank God Logan found her in time. Just not soon enough. Emerson still carries a faint bruise on her cheek from where that son of a bitch slapped her. The guy is lucky he's still alive. Logan told me Riggs handled the prospect. But he also said Quinn disappeared from the clubhouse not long after the prospect was sent away, and when he returned an hour later his knuckles were busted up. One guess as to what he did. "I know the guys are feeling like shit about the whole situation too. The club would never stand for a woman to be treated such a way," I continue.

"Seriously, I'm fine. And I know the guys would never allow something like that to happen. I promise I'm okay. It's not the first time I've had to deal with scum, and it won't be the last. Now enough apologizing and let's talk about why you're here," she scolds. Though I want to question her further by what she means when she said she's had to deal with scum before, the look on her face tells me she doesn't want me to press.

Deciding to bite the bullet and just come out with it, I tell her. "I want to adopt Baby Doe." I wait for a second to see what her response is going to be, but when I look over at her, she has a big smile on her face. Emerson does not seem to be the least bit shocked at my statement.

"I knew by the second day you spent with her this was going to be the outcome," she tells me.

"What? You did?"

Emerson smiles behind her cup. "I did. The second day you visited her, I snuck up to the NICU to check on you. You didn't see me, but I watched you. When you were holding her, the way you were looking down at her and she was looking up at you, I knew that you two belong to each other. You two meeting was meant to be. Her mother abandoned her, you were lost, and you both found each other."

For the second time this morning I'm crying. Emerson sets her cup down on the table and inches closer to me on the sofa hugging me. Pulling away from her, I use the sleeve of my shirt to wipe my eyes. I'm thankful I decided to forgo makeup today. "Do you have any advice as to what my first step should be?" I ask.

Standing, Emerson walks into the kitchen and over to the counter where her cell phone is. "I have a friend that works with Social Services. I'm going to call her and see about getting the ball rolling on you becoming a foster parent. The adoption process could be lengthy and if you were able to foster, then at least the baby would be able to stay with you and Logan during that time."

Suddenly feeling nervous about my chances of being accepted, I ask, "What about the club? No way will the state approve us with Logan being a member of an MC."

"Don't you worry about that. My friend owes me big time. She will come through for me on getting you accepted." Sagging with relief, I wait and listen as Emerson makes her call.

Later that evening I'm preparing dinner and waiting for

Emerson's call. When I left her apartment, she assured me that her friend was going to pull some strings and get Logan and I accepted. Hearing the front door open, I look over my shoulder and smile when I see Logan walking through. Striding into the kitchen, he takes his cut off and hangs it on the back of the barstool then walks up behind where I'm standing at the stove and wraps his arms around me and kisses my neck. His touch sends shivers down my spine.

"Hi, Angel," he rasps into the crook of my neck.

"Hi," I whisper back just before his mouth claims mine.

"You get things sorted out today?"

"I hope so. I went to see Em this morning, and she called in a favor. She said our best bet is to become foster parents first, that way Bree could live with us while we file for adoption."

"That's good, babe. When will we hear something back?"

"Em said she'd call me soon. I'm nervous Logan. What if they say no? I can't stand the thought of Bree getting shuffled from one foster home to the next, or her ending up with bad people," I choke out.

"Don't let those negative thoughts creep inside your head. Everything will work out." Blowing out a breath, I allow my body to relax back into Logan's frame.

"You're right. No need in me getting worked up until there is something to be worked up about." Glancing around the kitchen and in the living room, Logan asks, "Where's Sofia?"

"She's staying the night with her friend Lucy. They're working on a history paper," I tell him.

A moment later we both turn our heads toward the door when we hear the bell ring. "Can you let your dad in while I finish dinner?"

Logan strides to the front door and greets his father. I'm pulling the enchiladas out of the oven when they both walk into the kitchen. Taking the oven mitts off and setting them on the counter I turn to greet Demetri. That man is a sight. His dark hair with the slightest touch of grey on the sides and those trademark green and blue eyes. I love my husband, but I can appreciate a good-looking man. "How are you doing, Demetri?" I ask, kissing him on his cheek.

"I am well, Krasavitsa *beautiful*," he says, giving my arm a gentle squeeze.

"Why don't you two go sit out on the deck, and I'll bring you a beer. Dinner will be ready in about fifteen minutes."

"Thanks, babe," Logan says and kisses my temple before leading his dad out to the deck.

An hour later and nearly a whole casserole dish of enchiladas gone, Logan, his dad and I are sitting by the fire pit with full stomachs while drinking beer. I'm sitting in Logan's lap with my head resting on his chest and enjoying the rumble of his voice as his and Demetri's conversation flows freely. I'm brought out of my daze when I hear my cell phone ringing from inside.

Sliding off Logan's lap, I make my way inside to answer my call. Seeing Emerson's name on the screen, I respond immediately. "Em?" On the other end of the line, I hear her deep sigh and my gut is telling me she has bad news. "Just tell me Em," I urge.

"You and Logan were accepted."

Closing my eyes, I let out the breath I was holding. "Thank God," I breathe.

"But it's going to take at least six months for all the paperwork to process," she states next, dropping the bomb.

Just like that, my hopes are shattered. "Six months!" I nearly shout, and seconds later Logan is by my side.

"I'm sorry, Bella. My friend was able to get you accepted, but she still has to go through her supervisor. She did try everything she could," Emerson's voice sounds pained.

"It's okay, Em. I know you did everything you could. I am grateful for your help."

"We'll figure something out, Bella."

I don't want her to feel even worse than she already does. "You've done enough Em; seriously, you're a good friend. I'll talk with Logan, and we'll see what happens next."

I let out another deep sigh, "Okay, I'll call you tomorrow."

Hanging up the phone, I turn to Logan and bury my face in his chest. "We were accepted as foster parents but will have to wait at least six months," I say through muffled sobs.

Logan runs his palms up and down my arms trying to comfort me, "We'll figure something out, Angel."

"Son? Is everything alright?" I hear Demetri ask.

When I look up at Logan, I see him silently ask me if it's okay to tell his father what's going on, and I give a slight nod allowing him to confide in his dad.

"Bella and I have decided to adopt. As I was just discussing with you earlier, Bella has been volunteering at the hospital. She has been visiting a baby girl who was abandoned by her mother. The baby has come to mean somethin' to Bella, and we have decided to see about making her ours," he says.

"That's wonderful news, yes?" Demetri smiles.

Shaking his head, Logan continues. "It is, but adoption can take a while, so Bella's friend pulled some strings and got us accepted as foster parents, only it could take up to six months for everything to be finalized."

"I see," Demetri remarks, understanding our dilemma. Reaching into his suit jacket, Logan's father pulls out his cell phone. After tapping on the screen, he holds it up to his ear. A second later he begins to speak. "Donovan, find out who the head of Montana Social Services is. Logan and his wife have some paperwork that needs to be pushed to the top of the pile by the end of the day tomorrow. Call me when it's taken care of."

Demetri ends his call, and I'm standing here stunned while

Logan has a huge smile on his face. *What the hell just happened?*
"Wh...what did you just do?" I ask, barely able to find my words.

"Helped my son and daughter-in-law make me a Deda *grandfather.*"

Unable to hold back sobs, I'm scooped into Logan's arms and he whispers into my ear, "You see, Angel, I told you it would all work out."

9

LOGAN

Prez showed up this morning looking like he'd been through hell. He briefly pulled me to the side just before church letting me know about a text he received from an unknown number claiming to be Grace. She was letting him know she wouldn't be coming back to town for awhile, if at all. He didn't disclose any other details except for the fact it's not settling too well with him. Therefore, we have another issue on our hands to investigate.

The Louisiana chapter ended up staying an extra day longer than expected to make sure there wouldn't be any fallout from the asshole who tried to harm Emerson. However, they did come here for more than a good time. We're all heading into church so they can get on the road today.

"Jake, good to see ya, brother. You missed a good party the other night," Riggs stops just before entering the room and shakes Prez's hand.

"Riggs. Sorry, I had to miss it," Jake replies, his tone tired and a little scratchy.

"No worries. Next time you come down south, I'll make sure

you don't miss out," Riggs places his hand on Prez's shoulder telling him.

"I'll hold you to it, brother," Prez tells him. And they walk into the room.

Once everyone files in, the meeting starts. We run over the usual bullshit before Riggs, and his other officers fill us in on matters down south. It turns out they are having a bit of a problem with a couple of local gangs starting turf wars in the area, and one is pushing some heavy shit. Things sound like they are starting to get bad, just as Riggs stated yesterday.

Leaning back in his chair Prez asks, "What do you need us to do?"

"I'm aware you've gotten out of the gun trade, but I need to get my hands on a few things. My list of items is particular to my style and my taste," Riggs tells him.

Prez drums his knuckles on the table a few beats as he thinks. His eyes cut to mine. "You think your old man could help us out?"

I nod my head. More than confident my dad will make good on anything, I reply, "I can give him a call."

Pulling a piece of paper from his pocket, Fender slides it across the table. Jake unfolds and reads it before handing it to me. It's a list of materials and supplies. Military grade equipment mostly. *Shit*. Riggs was serious about being particular and hard to get.

M40A5/6/7 Sniper Rifle

NVDs (night vision goggles)

M4A1s

Just to name a few.

I lift my eyes from the paper. With a raised eyebrow I look at him.

His shoulders shrug, "I'm a bit of a prepper. I like being ready for anything. Including war," he admits.

"The moment you need our presence you let me know. We'll ride down and help clean house," Prez tells him.

"Good to know, brother. For right now I think watching them is best. I don't want to make them jumpy. Not yet anyway."

I fold the paper and slide it back to Prez. I'll let him and my dad sort out the details like they used to. The rest of church is hashing out plans for a run and sparking interest in the club. Gain a few recruits throughout the rest of the year. See if we can build our numbers. When it's over, we gather outside.

Riggs, Fender and Kiwi gear up to head out, minus one prospect.

"Had a good time. You come on down when you get the chance, and we will show you how we do it in Louisiana. Ya?" Riggs announces as he throws his leg over his bike and slides his shades over his eyes.

"You got it," I tell him.

"You bring dat pretty woman of yours too." He smirks.

Aside from the incident with Emerson, the weekend went well. Everyone had a good time and took care of business at the same time. Once they've cleared the property line, the guys and I head back inside. I pull my phone from my pocket and check the time. Gabriel walks up and plants his large hand on my shoulder. "Today is the day?"

He's referring to the first day I'll be meeting Breanna. I'd like to say I'm fine; the truth is I'm nervous as fuck. Bella has had more time to bond with her and get to know her little personality. I've watched her settle into the mom role, and it looks so beautiful on her. I want that too. I want to feel what she is feeling. I want the baby to connect with me. What if she doesn't? What if I don't feel the connection Bella talks about all the time? I want kids more than anything. I don't care how that comes about, but what if I've missed that crucial time where we can form our bond. "I meet Bella at the hospital in an hour," I tell him.

"It's the best feeling ever, brother," Gabriel confesses. One last pat and he walks away. Walking into the kitchen, I head to the cabinet and grab a coffee mug from inside. Pouring the coffee into the cup, I carry it to the table and take a seat next to Reid whose nursin' his own as he types away on his laptop. Whatever he's doing he has an intense look on his face.

Curiosity gets the best of me, so I ask him, "What up?"

Pausing he picks up his coffee and takes a drink. "Prez asked me to see what I could dig up on Grace."

I guess he isn't entirely convinced that Grace wanted to leave. I'm not entirely convinced myself. I rub and stretch my neck trying to work the tension out of it. I feel Reid studying me. With a raise of my brow, indicating he needs to speak whatever it is that's on his mind, he finally spills.

"It was unexpected. The connection I have with Ava. She may be a part of my brother—my blood, but I wasn't there for the first four years of her life. We were strangers, but she accepted me—loved me just as I loved her from day one. Hearing her call me daddy for the first time was one of the most defining moments in my life," he tells me.

I don't say anything. He wouldn't have mentioned a thing if he couldn't have read me right. The whole club knows everything at this point. Our loss is their loss. Our goals, dreams, and determination mingle with their support as they do everything they can to help them become a reality.

I gulp down the last of my coffee and stand. "I'll see ya later," I tell Reid as I keep my thoughts and emotions in check.

A short drive later I'm pulling into the parking lot at the hospital. Bella is sitting on a bench located near the entrance of the hospital waiting on me and scrolling through pictures on her phone as I stride up behind her.

She looks up from her phone. Standing, she tucks it into her back pocket and wraps her arms around my waist, burying her face into my chest. Her scent fills my senses and her touch instantly easing my nerves. I run my hands through her hair. Tilting her head back I lower mine and kiss her lips.

Licking my taste from her bottom lip, she peers at me through her lashes. "You ready?" she asks as she runs her fingers through my hair.

"I'm ready."

Heads turn as we make our way down the hallway before stopping at the nurses' station.

"Hi, Bella," a nurse in pink scrubs greets her as she steals another look my way, which causes Bella to smile.

"Hey, Emily. Breanna ready for us?"

A smile lifts at the nurse's lips, "She is. That little outfit you brought by yesterday is too sweet on her. Sign in and follow me," she says.

I sign my name to the paper and then I am given a visitor pass before we are led through double doors.

"She was moved to the regular nursery earlier this morning. I have a private room set up for you both," the nurse says and leads us past the giant nursery window. About that time a doctor is reading a chart in his hands as he passes by, lifts his head, and stops us.

"Mrs. Kane. I'm glad I ran into you. I was just with the hospital's social worker assigned to this case. She got a call from her supervisor downtown. I'm pleased to hear you'll be fostering Breanna."

We are both aware that someone should be bringing all the necessary paperwork by sometime this week. It's nice to know things are moving along smoothly. I have my dad to thank for that.

"I'm sure you've already heard we moved her out of the NICU. She has improved so much since you've been coming in. I would say in another few days she should be ready to leave the hospital," he finishes telling her before glancing at me. "I apologize for not introducing myself. I'm Dr. Silver, you must be Mr. Kane." He offers his hand.

"I am," I remark.

"Then I don't need to tell you what an incredible woman you have here. Congratulations to you both. You'll make great parents," he finishes just as his name is called over the intercom system and he excuses himself.

The nurse takes us around the corner, and we enter the small room. Inside next to a rocking chair is a little hospital crib. My steps slow. I watch Bella walk up and reach in, picking up the baby. I vaguely hear the door click shut behind us.

I can't take my eyes off them. Bella carefully cradles a cooing baby swaddled in a pink blanket. The pure look of content and happiness radiates from her smiling face as she quietly talks to her.

"Hey, pretty girl. Someone wants to meet you," she softly speaks as she strokes the curly hair on top of Breanna's head.

With confidence, my woman walks up to me and places the tiny bundle in my arms. I look down on her little face. Her light blue eyes connect with mine. The moment I feel it is when her tiny hand wraps around my finger.

I'm done for.

A memory comes back to me.

The vision clear as the day I first had it; the day I asked Bella to marry me. The image of Bella sitting at the water's edge at our lake. Her belly swollen with my son, and a little girl running around with deep brown curls.

My worries fade.

All this time. Breanna was meant to be ours.

I didn't understand any of what Bella has been feeling, what Reid and Gabriel meant. Not until this exact moment. I raise my head to find Bella intently watching me. Tears softly fall over her cheeks. She knows. She knows this little girl has stolen my heart. I'm her daddy. She is my little girl.

"It's amazing, isn't it?" She reaches out and strokes our daughter's hair. "I didn't grow her in my womb, but she is mine. She is ours."

I reach out and pull her into my chest. Holding them both, I kiss the top of Bella's head. "I love you, Angel." I then place a gentle kiss on our daughter's forehead. "I love both of you."

10

BELLA

Everything with Breanna is happening so fast. Ever since Demetri stood in our living room the other night and made that phone call, things have been happening at warp speed. I can't believe she is coming home this week. I'm crazy nervous but excited at the same time.

Yesterday Logan met Bree for the first time. I could tell he was nervous, but as soon as I placed her in his arms, I knew he felt the same instant connection I did upon holding her for the first time. It was at that moment I knew without a shadow of a doubt she was our daughter. Now with only five days to prepare our home for a baby, I'm scrambling to get everything in order.

Last night I finally broke down and called my sister for reinforcements. She agreed to go shopping with me today. Alba texted me earlier saying she'd come to my house and pick me up since we'd be using her truck.

Now here I am pacing back and forth on my front porch slightly irritated because she is thirty minutes late.

"Babe, relax. You have plenty of time to get everything done," Logan stresses stepping out of the front door.

Sighing, I sit down on the front step and rest my elbows on my knees as I place my face into the palm of my hands. "I know, I'm just anxious is all. I want everything to be perfect for Bree."

Taking a seat next to me on the step, Logan wraps his arm around my shoulder and urges me into his chest then kisses me on top of my head. "It'll be okay, Angel. Stop stressing and take one step at a time. You're so focused on how much shit needs to be done and how little time you have that you're forgetting something important."

Looking up at his face I ask, "What am I forgetting?"

"To have fun. I want you to go with your sister today and savor this memory...this day. When you're picking out Bree's crib, remember you're buying our daughter's first bed. When you are buying her clothes, you are picking out our daughter's first outfit. When you are deciding what bottles to choose, remember those are the bottles you will spend countless amounts of hours feeding our daughter. I want you to stop worrying about your to-do list and focus on making memories. The first of many."

By the time Logan has finished his little speech some of my worries disappear. He's right. "I love you," I say, kissing him.

"I love you too, Angel."

Roughly four hours and three stores later, my sister and I are exhausted, but we managed to put a dent in my list. I was able to get all the furniture for the baby's room such as her crib, changing table, dresser, and rocking chair. All of which are being delivered to our house this afternoon. I called Logan at work, and he said he would have one of the guys go over to the house and wait for the delivery men to show up. "Do you mind if we stop by my place before taking you home?" Alba asks.

"Sure, is everything okay?"

"Yeah, I just need to give you something. I got you a gift."

"You didn't have to get me anything, Alba," I chastise.

"Oh, hush. Yes, I did," she argues back as we pull up in front of her and Gabriel's house.

Climbing out of Alba's truck, I follow her to the front door. Using her key, my sister unlocks the door. As soon as it swings open and she flicks the lights on, I hear a chorus of voices screaming.

"SURPRISE!"

I stand next to my sister stunned with my mouth hanging open. Lisa, Mila, Emerson, Leah, Sofia, and holy shit, even Leyna is here. I can't believe this. After a second, I'm finally able to find my words, and when I do, I turn to my sister who has a huge triumphant smile on her face.

"You little shit," I say to her, my smile matching hers.

Alba's living room has been decorated in pinks and purples. There is a big banner hanging on the mantle of the fireplace that says *IT'S A GIRL*.

"A baby shower. How did you do all this?" I ask, blinking back my tears.

"I started planning the moment you told me the news you were bringing Breanna home this week. I made a few calls and all the girls pitched in. You're going to be a mom, Bella. And we all want to celebrate with you," my sister tells me in a soft voice.

Pulling Alba to me, I hug the shit out of her and whisper in her ear, "I love you, baby sister."

After I have opened all the gifts and played the silly baby shower games my sister insisted on, we all sit and chat while eating cake and watch as Gabe makes a mess with his. He's wearing more cake than he is eating. There is a moment when we all look at each other in silence, and I know each one of us is thinking the same thing.

Grace.

I say a silent prayer that our friend is safe and returns to Polson where she belongs. None of us know anything about her past and I suspect there is a story there, but what I do know is Grace has come to mean a great deal to all of us.

"Alright, let's get this stuff loaded up in the truck so I can get Bella home. It's getting late, and we all know how Logan gets when he's away from his woman for too long," my sister announces bringing me out of my thoughts. Standing up from the sofa, I begin to go around the room and gather dirty plates and cups.

"Oh no you don't, Bella," Lisa chastises. "The guest of honor doesn't do the clean-up. You go home to your husband. We'll take care of this mess."

Knowing better than to argue with her, I do what she says. Once I've made my way around the room to pass out hugs and thank my friends for showing so much love and support, I follow Alba out to her truck so that she can take me home.

On the way to my house, my sister and I pass Quinn, Reid, and Gabriel on their bikes. "The guys must have come by for a beer after work," I wonder aloud.

"Probably," my sister agrees.

When we pull up to the house, Logan is sitting on the porch with a beer in his hand. Setting it down, he makes his way down the steps and around the back of the truck to unload my purchases from the day and my shower gifts. When I step out of my sister's vehicle, I hear the rumble of a motorcycle. Looking at the end of the driveway, I see Gabriel. He's sitting on his bike smoking a cigarette. It's starting to get dark outside, and I know he's waiting for Alba to follow her home.

Glancing at my sister she smiles and rolls her eyes. Gabriel is protective, and he doesn't like Alba out at night. She may act annoyed at times, but I know she secretly loves it. Giving my sister one last hug and grabbing the last of the bags out of the back seat, I use my free hand to wave to her as she starts her truck and makes her way down the driveway. Once she's turned onto the road, Gabriel gives Logan a nod before he falls in behind her.

"Come on, babe, let's get this shit inside." When we walk inside, Logan shuts the door behind me and sets the alarm. "Come on, Angel; I have something to show ya."

Without question, I follow him up the stairs and briefly admire his ass on the way up. When Logan looks over his shoulder at me, he smirks...*busted.* I smile and shrug my shoulders, what can I say? My man has a fine-looking ass.

When we make it to the end of the hallway, Logan pushes open the bedroom door that is across from ours. When he does the bag that was in my hand drops to the floor as I bring my hand up to my mouth. The sight in front of me is breathtaking. Taking a few more steps into the room, my eyes scan every single inch of it, taking in its perfection. The walls have been painted light lavender. All the furniture I bought and had delivered today has been put together. The crib I chose is white along with a dresser and changing table. Hanging on the window is some heather grey curtains and next to the window is the grey rocking chair I picked out.

Everything is in its place, just as I described to my sister as we walked through each store.

With every piece I picked out, I would tell her exactly where I wanted it in the nursery.

Alba must have relayed my detailed description back to Logan. I notice the things I didn't buy today. Toys and stuffed animals. A bookcase filled with children's books.

"From your sister," Logan tells me when I walk over to the bookcase and run my fingers along the spines.

"Of course, it is." I smile.

Walking up behind me, Logan pulls me into his chest. "When your sister told me what she had planned for you today, I called up the guys and had them come help me."

I turn my body into his arms so I can face him. "How did I get so lucky?"

"I'm the lucky one, Angel," Logan declares right before his mouth crashes down on mine.

Four days later, Logan and I are in my car on the way to the hospital to pick up Breanna. I look over my shoulder into the back seat at the empty car seat. The same car seat that next time we get in this car won't be empty any longer. I'm brought out of my thoughts when I feel Logan's warm hand clamp over the top of mine.

"Stop fidgeting, beautiful. Everything is going to be fine. My dad said the other day our paperwork is in order. A lady with Social Services will be at the hospital to sign off and finalize everything. We're bringing our daughter home today. I promise."

"I know. I just can't help but worry that something will go wrong. A part of me will keep worrying until the day comes when a judge makes her officially ours. I hate that we have to wait for months for it to happen. So many things can happen over a six-month period." I sigh.

"Yeah babe, a shit ton of stuff can happen, but we're going to focus on starting our family. Nothing else matters."

"No more dwelling on the what-ifs." Several minutes later we arrive at the hospital. I wait for Logan as he turns the car off, gets out and walks around to the passenger side and opens my door.

He holds out his hand. "You ready, Angel?"

Taking a deep cleansing breath and releasing it, I place my hand in his. "Yeah, let's do this."

Thirty minutes later Logan is holding a car seat with Breanna strapped in and we watch as the social worker signs on the dotted line. We are now officially Bree's foster parents. Next the doctor hands over the discharge papers along with an appointment card for her check-up she will need in two weeks.

"Best of luck Mr. and Mrs. Kane. I'll see you back here in two weeks," the doctor says with a handshake before walking off.

I turn my attention back to the social worker. "So, that's it?"

"Yes, Mrs. Kane that's it. You're free to take Breanna home." She smiles.

"Come on, Angel. Let's go home."

I look at my husband who is holding the car seat with our baby girl inside; I beam up at him and thread my fingers through his free hand. "Let's go home."

11

LOGAN

Hearing a cry coming from the baby monitor causes Bella and me both to stir from our sleep. "I'll get her," I whisper into Bella's ear as I untangle myself from her warm body.

"Are you sure?" she asks in a raspy, sleep filled voice.

"Yeah, Angel. I've got her. Go back to sleep." Getting out of bed, I grab my sweatpants and pull them on over my boxer briefs before making my way across the hallway to Bree's room. Walking up to her crib I grin when she spots me, and I see her eyes are laser focused on me and she immediately stops fussing. "Hi, pretty girl," I rumble and lean over her crib to carefully pick her up and bring her close to my chest. Breanna has been home for a week, and I still get nervous holding her. She's so tiny and delicate. She has been a good baby so far, and only fusses when she needs changing, is hungry, or simply needs to be held.

After going downstairs to the kitchen to make her a bottle, I bring her back up to her nursery. Sitting down in the rocking chair, I cradle Bree in the crook of my arm and watch as she greedily takes the bottle in her mouth. Before Bella, I never saw myself as a family man and I especially never saw myself with a little girl. And though the adoption is not final, Breanna is mine. I don't need a piece of paper to tell me different. I love this little girl fiercely. She may not have my blood, but she has my heart. I'll take care of and protect her until my last breath.

I hate that Bella's still worried something will go wrong with the adoption process, but with my father stepping in on our behalf, I know we have nothing to worry about. She will be ours. My father has even gone as far as to track down Breanna's birth mom. He wanted to ensure she signed over her rights and that she would not be a problem for us in the future. It turns out she wouldn't be a problem at all because she was found in a hotel a few towns over; dead from a heroin overdose, and no word on the birth father. I suspect the woman didn't even know who the father was. Police reports showed multiple prostitution arrests on her record as well. Bella and I know that one day when she is older, Bree will have questions, and we will do our best to always be honest with her and answer those questions the best we can.

Feeling her presence before she speaks, I cut my eyes over my shoulder and spy Bella standing in the doorway of the room. The glow of the moon coming through the large window of the nursery is casting light over her face. She looks so fuckin' beautiful standing there wearing my t-shirt and her hair is a wild mess of waves hanging over her shoulders. I am without a doubt the luckiest son of a bitch alive.

"Did we wake you, Angel?"

She shakes her head. "No, I couldn't go back to sleep, so I thought I'd come to see how you two were doing."

Slipping the bottle from Bree's mouth, I take a burp cloth and place it over my shoulder then bring her close to me and begin to pat her back lightly. The first time I fed Breanna, I didn't know I was supposed to burp her every so often during feedings. I ended up getting covered in spit up. When she threw up, it looked like something straight out of *The Exorcist.* I won't make that mistake again, although Bella got a good laugh at my expense.

Knowing Bella wants Bree, I stand up and motion for her to sit in the rocking chair. Once she settles, I pass the cloth to her and then lean forward to pass Bree to her carefully. Bella is a natural with her. You can see she was meant to be a mother. I love seeing the two of them bond. Without a doubt I fall more and more in love with my woman every day. Not wanting the moment to end, I walk over to the window in front of the chair and sit down on the floor leaning against the wall, stretching my legs out in front of me. We both sit in complete silence. Bella is keeping her eyes on our little girl as she rocks and quietly hums to her, and I continue to stare at my beautiful wife. I imprint the moment into my brain. It will go down in history as one of my most cherished memories.

The next morning Bella and I are at the kitchen table having coffee and breakfast when Sofia walks in. "Morning," she greets plucking a banana out of the fruit bowl on the counter. Sofia has been a big help this past week. The first two days Bree was home she was hardly home. Bella noticed Sofia seemed to be almost pulling away. We both began to worry about how she was taking it with us having a new addition to the family. Though Sofia is only a few years younger than Bella, I know Bella feels very protective and motherly toward her. It's just in her nature. Bella is an old soul and having grown up so fast the way she did with having to take care of her sister, she took on the same role with Sofia. So, on the second day of Sofia staying out all day, Bella confronted her. It turns out Sofia felt she needed to give us space and some alone time. She said she didn't want to be in the way. I'll admit it caused a pain in my chest to hear those words come out of her mouth. We love Sofia. She is a part of this family, and we've shown her as much. I had to remind her that this is her home too and would always be her home. She has never been in the way, nor will she ever be a burden.

"What do you guys think about having the family over today? Bree has been home a week, and I know everyone is anxious to come to see her," Bella says.

Sofia is the first to speak up. "Sounds like fun. Can I invite Leah and Sam?"

"Of course," Bella agrees. "I want to invite everyone. Can you call the guys Logan?" she asks.

"Yeah, Angel. I'll get everyone here. How about you write down what you want to cook, and Sofia and I will run to the store."

Thirty minutes later after calling the guys and telling them to get their asses to my place in two hours, Sofia and I are on our way to the grocery store. When she asked Bella earlier if she could invite Sam over, I decided to have her ride with me, so we could have a little talk about what was going on with the two of them. Don't get me wrong, I like Sam and he's a good kid, but protecting Sofia is my job. She's been through so much in her life already, and I don't want to see her go through anymore. I clear my throat. "I've noticed you've been hanging out with Sam a lot lately." I watch Sofia's cheeks turn pink, and she ducks her face. Pulling into a parking spot, I turn my truck off then turn toward her. Placing my finger under her chin, I coax her to look at me.

"We're just friends," she answers softly.

"But you like him more than friends?" I ask.

She shrugs. "It doesn't matter what I feel. Sam doesn't see me that way. Probably because I'm not good enough for him." Her statement and low opinion of herself pisses me off.

"Sofia, look at me," I demand. When her innocent brown eyes meet mine, I see sorrow, uncertainty, and unshed tears. "He's not good enough for you. There isn't a bastard out there who will ever be good enough to deserve you. I'm positive Sam sees you. He sees you as a hell of a lot more than I would like," I grind out. "And fair warning, when he man's up and makes his feelings known, he will have a long line of men ready to beat his ass if he breaks your heart. If Sam is the decent guy, I think he is, then he's just waiting for the right time, sweetheart. Now, let's go in this store and get what we came for before my woman starts blowing up my phone asking me what's takin' so long." Sofia lets out a watery chuckle. Opening the passenger door, she turns and looks over her shoulder at me.

"Thanks, Logan."

"Damn brothers, would you look at this shit," Quinn says with his arms raised and motioning around my backyard at all the activity going on when he walks up to me, Reid, and Gabriel. "Two years ago, we would've had a pool full of strippers. Now wherever I look I see kids and toys every-fuckin'-where."

Reaching up, I slap him on the back of the head. "Shut the fuck up, asshole."

"Alright, alright, I was only jokin' man. Seriously, I'm happy for you. Kids are fuckin' great. I can't wait to have me some. I want at least five," he declares.

"Good luck with that," Reid tells him. "You have to find a woman to put up with your ass first."

"Not a problem, brother. I already have the perfect baby momma in mind," Quinn tells us as his eyes cut over to Emerson who is sitting across the yard with the women.

There is one thing I know for sure about my brother, he is persistent. Like the rest of us when we want something, he goes after it and won't stop until he gets it. Quinn comes across as a goofy motherfucker, and he is, but he's also all heart. Quinn will lay down his life for anyone he cares about and put a bullet in your head if he sees you as a threat to his family.

As the evening winds down and the sun begins to set, I sit in my chair and look around at my family that surrounds me. Jake, Gabriel, Quinn, Reid, Nikolai, my father, Bennett and his wife Lisa, Bella, Alba, Emerson, Sofia, Leah, and Sam, Gabe and Ava who are playing in the yard, Val who is in her mama's arms and my daughter who is asleep in Bella's. This is the fucking life. At that moment, my brothers and I all meet each other's eyes, and at the same time we all lift our bottles toward each other in a silent, *hell yeah.*

12

BELLA

It's hard to believe that four months have gone by. Four entire months we have been a family of four. As I drink my coffee, I watch Breanna sitting in her stationary walker while she swings a plastic teether ring in the air. So far except for her being a little below average on the growth scale, her development is on schedule for her age. The doctors don't seem to think she will have any lasting effects from being born with drugs in her system. I can't begin to express how relieved Logan and I both were to hear that little bit of news last week when she had a follow-up appointment with her developmental specialist. To top it off, we got the call yesterday we have been waiting for. In a couple of days, our daughter will legally be ours.

Just like most days since bringing Breanna home, I'm spending time with my sister. I've stopped working at the shop for now, so I can completely devote my time to be a stay-at-home mommy. The choice not to work was much harder than I thought it would be. I've worked hard since I was sixteen and enjoyed what I was doing at the shop. Spending my days watching our daughter grow and discover the world around her has been so worth it.

"How are you feeling?" I ask my sister as she sinks back into her chair holding my sleeping niece in her arms. I know she has been up late into the night trying to finish graphics for authors the past week. I'm proud of her. Alba has made a name for herself and has started to obtain quite a few clients since starting her cover design business.

"Like I need a vacation," she answers with a yawn.

"I don't see how you do it. You have two little ones and still manage to do everything you do," I respond. I admire my sister. She is such a good mother.

"You look tired today, long night?"

"Bree slept all night. It has been for a couple of weeks now, but I do feel tired. To top it off I put on my favorite pair of jeans this morning and couldn't button the damn things. I'm getting fat," I tell her. To be honest, I can't fit into any of my jeans. I've been living in leggings for a month now. Taking Bree from the walker, I place her on my lap. Reaching behind me, I retrieve the diaper bag and grab a cloth to wipe a little dribble from Bree's mouth. When I'm through fussing over my baby girl happily playing in my lap, I look up. "What?" I inquire because Alba has a look on her face I can't decipher.

"Could you be pregnant?"

"What? No."

Standing she bends and places her sleeping daughter into the pack 'n play, "You say you're tired and you can't fit into your clothes. Have you felt nauseous at all?"

I think back. "No."

"Then how do you know? You could be. I know you've had irregular menstrual cycles since the miscarriage." Alba's eyes soften as soon as the word leaves her lips and I feel a physical squeeze on my heart. "But you can still get pregnant."

I haven't given it much thought. She's right about my cycle being off since then. The doctor said it was normal to experience cycle changes due to the stress of losing the baby, so I haven't attributed it to any other reason.

"Are you and Logan still trying? Are you preventing it from happening?" she asks.

My body tingles all over. Could I be? Alba walks to her purse which is sitting on the kitchen table, then walks back toward me holding out a package I know all too well. A pregnancy test.

"Here. Only one way to know for sure, right?"

"Should I even ask why you have one of those in your purse?" I raise my eyebrow at her.

She shrugs, "I'm content with the two we have for the moment, but the man is determined."

I can't do anything but shake my head and smile. I swap Bree for the test and walk to the bathroom. I take care of the deed and set the stick on the counter. A soft tap on the door reminds me to breathe again. Opening the door, I let my sister in.

"I laid Bree down with Valentina, she was starting to fall asleep. Gabe is sitting in his playpen playing with his toys." She peers past my shoulder, "Well?" my sister inquires about the test sitting on the counter behind me.

"I'm afraid to look. What if I am? What if I miscarry again? What if I'm not?" I confess the mess of emotions stirring inside of me. I'm scared to let myself hope.

"You want me to look first?" Alba asks.

Holding back tears, I nod my head. She brushes past me and picks up the pregnancy stick and looks down at it. I do my best to judge her expression. She has none. My stomach sinks.

Exhaling she turns and faces me. "You're pregnant." She flips the stick so that the digital window is visible.

Pregnant.

For a moment I can't form a coherent thought. Not until my sister touches my arm. I blink and look at her. Tears pool in my eyes and I blink them away. "Oh my god," I murmur and have to sit down on the edge of the tub to keep from falling. I'm pregnant. I'm going to have a baby.

She walks over and sits beside me. "Don't let yourself go there. You need to be positive about this. Let's go call the doctor and get you in to confirm everything."

I lean my head back and steady my breathing. Repeating over and over in my head, everything will be okay. Getting up, I walk back into the living room and retrieve my phone. The living room is silent. All three kids fast asleep.

A few minutes later, due to a cancellation, I have an appointment this afternoon in two hours. Sofia soon appears around the corner shortly after hearing the front door open and close. *Perfect timing.* "Hey, Sofia. Can you watch the kids? I need my sister to take me to the doctor," I ask her.

Placing her bag on the chair beside her, she gives me a concerned look. "Is everything okay?"

I drop my phone into my purse before sitting down on the couch joining Alba. "I need to have a pregnancy test done," I confess. "But I don't want to go alone."

A broad smile spreads across her face. "Of course I'll watch the kiddos." She plops down on the couch next to me, "This is crazy. So, you think you might be pregnant?" she questions hopefully.

I shrug my shoulders worried and unsure about everything. I am repeating what my sister said before Sofia tries to comfort me. *Think positively.*

"If it's meant to be, it will be," Sofia says.

Now I'm sitting in the exam room with Alba by my side, doing my best to stay positive. Maybe I should have called Logan, but I want to know for sure before I tell him. I don't want to get his hopes up.

"Mrs. Kane, your test came back positive, so let's look at you and baby and see just how far along you are," my doctor says after entering the room. The nurse who follows her begins preparing me by applying the cold gel to my stomach, then turns off the light as the doctor takes her seat. My sister can't stop smiling beside me. I won't allow myself to get excited just yet. I hold my breath.

"Okay," she says as she places the ultrasound wand onto my lower abdomen and moves it around. "There he or she is." She points to the computer screen.

I stare at the image. "I'm pregnant," I bring my hand to cover my mouth and fight the urge to cry.

"No doubt that you are indeed pregnant, and almost four months along by the looks of things."

"Holy shit!" I loudly whisper. I look down at my stomach which is a little pudgy. I thought I was overeating because I'm at home all day. "What about the spotting I've had the past few months?" I ask her with worry.

"It's normal to have some spotting early in pregnancy. You'll be monitored closely due to your history, but as far as I can see you and baby look good. Congratulations!" She smiles.

After cleaning the gel from my abdomen, I sit up as the doctor turns and hands me the pictures.

"Here's the baby's first selfie and a prescription for prenatal vitamins and some extra iron since your blood work showed your levels were a bit low. If you want to schedule a 3D sonogram to call the office and we'll get you set up."

I'm still at a loss for words while she continues to talk, and my fear is still very present.

"Bella," she addresses me personally. "Everything looks perfect. You've made it past the mark of your last pregnancy. Go home. Share the good news with your husband."

I can't believe we are going to have a baby. I reach down and place my hand on my belly and leave it there on my drive home.

"How do you plan on telling Logan?" Alba inquires as she drives us back to my place.

A smile spreads across my face. "Tomorrow after we legally become Breanna's parents."

***

Still in bed, I stretch and moan before strong arms pull my body close, wrapping me in a warm hug.

"Today's the day, Angel." Logan's breath dances across my ear causing my skin to prickle. Today is the day we legalize adoption. Today is also the day I give Logan his surprise. He knew I was hiding something from him when he came home last night. He tried to pry it out of me. Even used sex to try and make me cave. I stayed strong and told him I had a surprise for him, and he would have to wait until today. "Forever. She will be ours forever." I snuggle further into his embrace.

"How much longer are you going to make me wait for this surprise of yours?" He rubs his hand down over my hip before slipping it under my shirt and palming my breast. He starts to pepper kisses down the back of my neck.

"You have to wait a little while longer," I moan when he lightly rolls my nipple between his thumb and forefinger. Moving, he hovers his body above mine. Without thought, I spread my legs letting him settle between them. Before things get any further, Breanna makes herself known with her jibber playing through the baby monitor sitting on my nightstand. Logan smiles. She has stolen his heart. She has her daddy wrapped around her little finger. He presses his lips to mine.

"I'll get her. Why don't you go start some coffee," he says playfully.

Mornings have become his time with our daughter. I often lay and listen to the monitor while he sits and talks to her. Already telling her she can't date until she turns thirty or that he will beat any boy who breaks her heart. I lift my head from my pillow and give him a soft kiss. Breanna having waited long enough starts to fuss. Putting aside the want for one another, Logan climbs out of bed.

Soon after eating lunch we load up and head toward downtown. In less than an hour, we will go before the judge in family court. Logan reaches over and grabs my hand. We've been riding in silence with only the occasional babble from Breanna as Sofia plays with her in the back seat. Several Harleys fall in behind us. Twisting, I look through the rear window to see who I already knew I would see. Our family. Jake and the rest of the guys along with my sister behind them in her truck followed by Mila in her vehicle.

Standing outside the courthouse when we pull into a parking spot is Logan's brother Nikolai. He walks toward us while I try to unload Breanna.

"Glad you could make it," Logan says, closing the car door behind him.

"Wouldn't have missed your and Bella's big day," Nikolai says. Slinging the diaper bag over my shoulder, I snuggle Breanna in my arms, and we walk into the building along with everyone else.

Logan and I sit at a table before an older, grey-haired judge and our lawyer stands. After going through the swearing-in process, we run through stating our names, address, and occupation before our lawyer speaks.

"Your Honor, we're here today in the matter of the adoption of Breanna," our lawyer addresses the judge.

"I see we have a room full." The judge smiles, then addresses Logan and me directly, "Are you two prepared for what lies ahead? Are you prepared to take care of her until the legal age of eighteen?"

"Your honor, we'll take care of her for the rest of her life. She'll never want for anything," Logan declares.

The judge looks down at the papers he's shifting in his hands before picking up a pen he begins to write, "Mr. Kane, I have no doubt she will be well loved and cared for. Your caseworker has had nothing but good things to say about you and your wife." Lifting his head, he asks, "Mrs. Kane, could you please tell the court the full name of your daughter to be recorded."

My stomach flutters as excitement takes over. "Breanna Rose Kane, your honor," I say proudly. Reaching for her daddy, I pass Breanna to Logan. Logan's mom meant the world to him, so Breanna's middle name honors that love.

Rising from his seat, the judge makes his way to us, "Congratulations Mr. and Mrs. Kane." He hands Breanna a fuzzy brown teddy bear, which she eagerly grasps hold of in her hands. The room erupts in applause from our family. Reaching out, my husband and the judge shake hands.

"I wish your family all the best," he proclaims.

We're in the middle of taking a few pictures with the judge when I whisper to Logan, "Are you ready for your surprise?"

He pulls me into his side. "Surprise me."

I glance around the room to catch my sister and Sofia eagerly waiting for me to reveal my secret. I lean on my tiptoes and whisper in his ear, "I'm pregnant."

13

LOGAN

It takes me a minute to process what Bella said when her warm breath whispers in my ear, and now she is patiently waiting for me to react to the news.

"Logan? Did you hear me?"

Still holding my daughter, I focus my attention on my woman. "Are you sure?" I ask her. Swiping a tear from under her eye, she nods.

"I'm four months pregnant," she clarifies.

Holy shit. Just when I thought my life couldn't get any better, Bella proves otherwise. Placing my palm on her cheek, I lean in and claim her mouth, kissing her. Everything I ever wanted or needed in my life is right here in one room—my woman, our daughter Breanna, Sofia, my father and brother, and my club. And now I'm going to be a dad again in another five months. My life has come full circle. Nothing in my life feels unfinished. I'm over the fuckin' moon in love with the beautiful woman standing in front of our daughter whom I'm holding in my arms and me. Not being able to contain what I'm feeling I look toward our family still gathered at the back of the room. "We're having a baby!" I shout, and the courthouse erupts into a fury of cheers.

Turning to face my woman, I tell her, "Seems like there is only one thing left to do, beautiful."

"What's that?" she asks, smiling.

Before I can answer, Jake's voice booms from behind me.

"Party at the clubhouse!"

Chuckling, I pull Bella into my side and we follow our family out of the courthouse. "The only thing left to do, Angel, is celebrate."